THE GENTLEMEN OF 16 JULY

Other Books by Ken Follett

Eye of the Needle
Triple
Key to Rebecca

The Gentlemen

A Work of Narrative Nonfiction by

René Louis Maurice

and

Ken Follett

of 16 July

Arbor House
New York

Published in the United States of America by Arbor House Publishing Company and in Canada by Fitzhenry & Whiteside, Ltd.

Library of Congress Catalog Card Number: 80-52012

ISBN: 0-87795-298-1

Manufactured in the United States of America

12 11 10 9 8 7 6 5 4 3 2 1

Contents

	Prologue	ix
1	The Man Behind the Heist	20
2	Spaggiari Makes his Plans	33
3	A Jealous Wife	47
4	Getting In	63
5	Getting Out	80
6	The Investigation Begins	92
7	The Clues Come In	105
8	Spaggiari and the CIA	123
9	Spaggiari is Arrested	131
10	Spaggiari "Knowingly Destroys a Vehicle"	147
	Epilogue	159

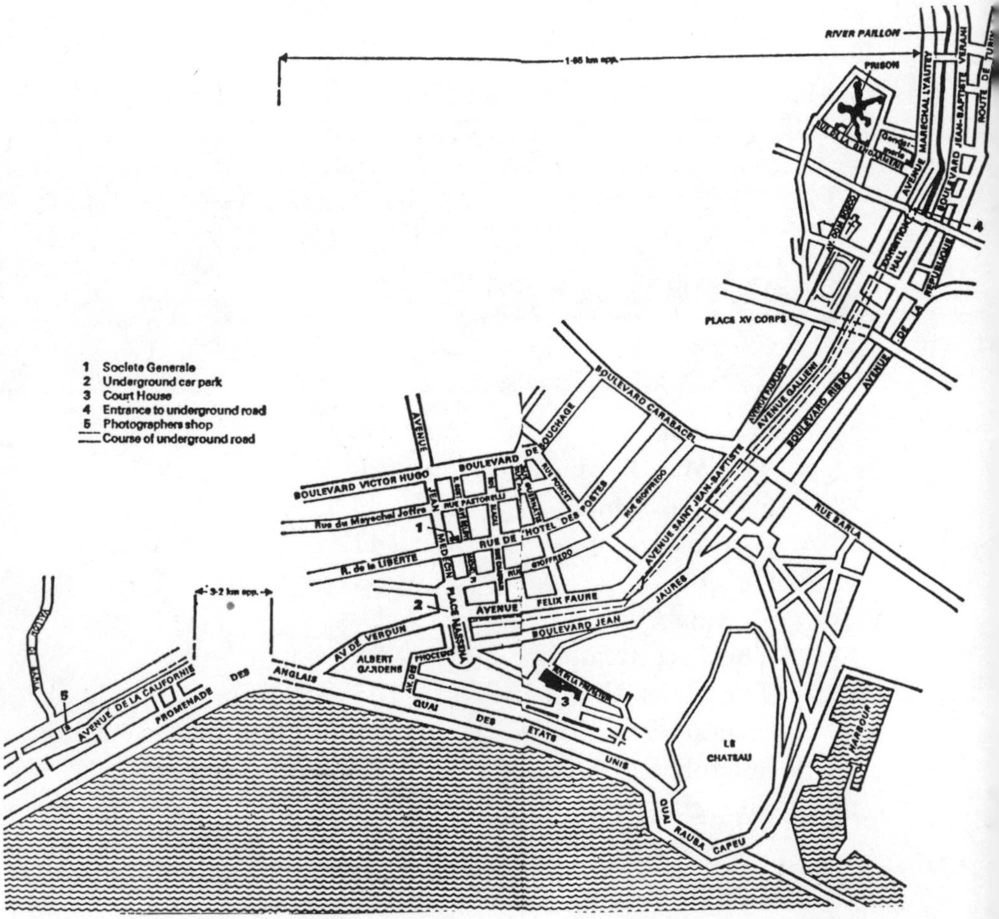
1 Societe Generale
2 Underground car park
3 Court House
4 Entrance to underground road
5 Photographers shop
Course of underground road
RIVER PAILLON
PRISON
1·65 km app.
3·2 km app.
PLACE XV CORPS
BOULEVARD CARABACEL
BOULEVARD VICTOR HUGO
BOULEVARD DUBOUCHAGE
AVENUE JEAN MEDECIN
RUE PASTORELLI
R. de la LIBERTE
RUE DE L'HOTEL DES POSTES
AVENUE FELIX FAURE
BOULEVARD JEAN JAURES
AVENUE SAINT JEAN-BAPTISTE
AVENUE GALLIENI
BOULEVARD RISSO
AVENUE DE LA REPUBLIQUE
AVENUE MARECHAL LYAUTEY
BOULEVARD JEAN-BAPTISTE VERANI
ROUTE DE TURIN
EXHIBITION HALL
RUE BARLA
PLACE MASSENA
AV DE VERDUN
ALBERT GARDENS
PROMENADE DES ANGLAIS
AVENUE DE LA CALIFORNIE
QUAI DES ETATS UNIS
QUAI RAUBA CAPEU
LE CHATEAU
HARBOUR

Prologue

UN "COUP" MONUMENTAL
—headline in *Nice-Matin,* 21 July 1976

IT WAS going to be a hot day.

The sun rose at eight minutes past six, and by breakfast time the town was sweltering. The holidaymakers took their *petit déjeuner* on shaded balconies; the motorists opened the roofs of their convertibles; the waiters lowered canopies over pavement cafés. The early risers were already on the pebble beach; slender brown girls took off their bikini tops to reveal slender brown breasts, and the locals looked on with unconcealed lust while the visitors pretended that topless sunbathing was nothing new to *them.* Along the promenade—a six-lane highway—the traffic roared past, polluting the warm Mediterranean air.

It was going to be hot for the holidaymakers, and for the motorists, and for the waiters; and it was going to be especially hot for Pierre Bigou. The thermometer would rise past eighty-six degrees Fahrenheit, but for Monsieur Bigou it would be much hotter.

Bigou was controller in chief of the main branch of the Société Générale bank at 8 Avenue Jean Médecin, in Nice, France. For him July 19, 1976 started out like a normal Monday morning. The high-ceilinged main hall of the bank was cool and hushed as the shirt-sleeved tellers prepared to receive their first customers when the doors opened at 8:30.

At 8:28 he checked his watch against the large clock on the wall in the main hall, then went into his office, leaving the door open, and began to read the morning paper. He had been with the bank for many years, he had reached a very senior position, and there was nobody to tell *him* off for reading the paper during working hours.

Van Impe had won the sixty-third Tour de France cycle race. The American space lab Viking I was on course for Mars. The weather forecast was warm and sunny. Big deal.

It was St. Arsene's Day, but there is no connection between Arsene—a perfectly respectable Catholic saint—and Arsene Lupin, the French Robin Hood, the patron saint of gentleman thieves.

At exactly 8:30 two bank functionaries passed

Bigou's door and went down the stairs to the vault. The chore of opening the vault door every morning was rotated among the bank's lesser employees, and this week it was their turn. Each carried a large key stamped "F.B."—for Fichet-Bauche, France's largest manufacturer of locks and safes.

The pair of steel doors at the foot of the stairs slid smoothly into the thick concrete walls. So far, so good.

Inside was another steel door, and this one was rather special. Fifty years old, three feet thick, and weighing twenty tons, it was believed to be immune even to a laser. The directors of the bank had had discussions with their insurance company, Lloyds of London, about installing a modern alarm system—and the two parties had agreed that the mighty door was so impenetrable that the modern paraphernalia of hidden cameras and trembler alarms and photoelectric sensors would be superfluous. One customer who rented a safe-deposit box in the vault had complained about the lack of alarms, but the man was a retired policeman who read too many whodunits, and nobody listened.

At 8:34 the two men simultaneously inserted their keys. The mechanism, made with old-fashioned craftsmanship, consisted of two sets of interlocking rods. Once the keys were in, the men disengaged the rods by operating three large wheels set on the door: each wheel was rotated a quarter-turn to the right for the horizontal rods, then a quarter-turn to the left for the vertical rods. As they went through the elaborate procedure the men could hear from inside the door the faint sounds of the mechanism unlocking.

At 8:35 the door was unlocked, and one of the men gave it the final gentle push which would open it wide.

Nothing happened.

The twenty-ton door refused to budge.

That was when the day began to go wrong for Pierre Bigou.

THE TWO men looked at each other, shrugged and started again.

Two keys in.

Wheel number 1: a quarter-turn to the left, a quarter-turn to the right.

Wheel number 2: the same.

Wheel number 3: the same.

One of the men whispered: "Open Sesame."

A gentle push.

Nothing.

A voice said: "What's going on?"

The men turned to see a customer standing on the stairs, watching them. "It's nothing," one of them replied. "The door's sticking a little."

The customer grinned. "If you can't get in, at least we can be sure there's no chance of a robbery."

The two men smiled thinly and went through the routine a third time. By this time there was a small crowd on the stairs. The sarcastic remarks began to irritate the two bank officials, but they bore the teasing stoically, for the Société Générale is an old-established bank, and the customer is always right.

At 8:50 they admitted defeat. The door was stuck. They apologized to the waiting customers and went upstairs to inform their superiors.

The temperature was seventy-seven degrees Fahrenheit, and rising.

THE BANK'S *directeur*—manager—came down personally to apologize to the waiting customers. Jacques Guenet was a reassuring figure: sixty years old, powerfully built, well-known as vice-president of the Nice Rugby Club, he had what the French call *nerfs solides*—nerves of steel.

He smiled regretfully and spoke to the customers in a quiet, even voice. It was dreadfully inconvenient, he agreed, but a jammed door was not the end of the world, now was it? The specialists would be here within minutes to deal with the door, but he could not say how long the job would take.

As he ushered them back up the stairs, he said: "May I suggest you come back at two o'clock this afternoon? I'm sure everything will be done by then. This is just a little hitch—no doubt the heat has caused it . . ."

When he returned to the door Pierre Bigou, his deputy, was watching the two officials try the lock one last time. Neither Guenet nor Bigou was unduly worried: the lock had jammed once before during its fifty-year life, and a locksmith had unjammed it with a drop of oil.

The functionaires went through the motions for the umpteenth time, with the same result.

At nine o'clock Pierre Bigou returned to his office, picked up the phone and dialed 809761, the local office of Fichet-Bauche. The number was engaged. He glanced at his newspaper for a moment. Two German tourists had been shot, and a pimp had been paid two hundred forty thousand francs for a whore. Bigou, who had been nicknamed St. Peter by a disrespectful young employee, shuddered inwardly.

Nice in the seventies was unpleasantly reminiscent of the Chicago of the thirties. Mayor Jacques Médecin had given the town a facelift, but he had been unable to prevent its taking over from Marseilles as the international narcotics market. The *milieu*—the underworld—was divided into two warring factions, the Italians and the Corsicans, and in one two-year period twelve nightclub owners were murdered. On the Promenade des Anglais you could buy anything from a couple of hits of cocaine to a male prostitute. People said it was the most corrupt town in France.

Bigou shuddered again—so much crime! Was it possible that the jammed vault door . . . No, there would be signs: no one could have opened that door without leaving marks.

No one could have opened that door, period.

Even the insurers had thought so, and they were

never slow to recommend improved security.

Bigou picked up the phone and dialed again. This time it was answered.

"Hello—is that the Fichet-Bauche office? It's the Société Générale bank here. Can you send someone over very urgently? . . . No, the lock seems to be working, but the door is jammed . . . I'll be waiting for you."

At 9:15 a black and yellow Renault 4L pulled up in the Avenue Jean Médecin. The name "Fichet-Bauche" was lettered on the doors. Bigou gave a sigh of relief. Soon his troubles would be over.

BIGOU AND Guenet went down the stairs with the two locksmiths from Fichet-Bauche. The specialists seemed confident and self-assured as they went up to the vault door and examined it. Seeing no superficial clues, they asked for total silence then inserted the two keys. Moving with painful caution, they went through the unlocking procedure, listening carefully to the mechanism with heads cocked, looking for all the world like a pair of birds waiting for a worm.

Finally one of them turned to Guenet. "The lock is working perfectly. I can assure you that there is nothing wrong with the mechanism—the tumblers are moving quite freely."

There was a moment's silence. Guenet said: "Well?"

The locksmith shrugged.

"So why won't the door open?" Guenet said.

The locksmith said: "The only thing I can think of is that something is blocking it from the inside."

The banker stared at the locksmith in disbelief. It was unthinkable. He mumbled: "No, I can't believe that."

He turned around, and saw the staircase was thronged with curious employees. "Go back to work," he said irritably. "I don't want to see anyone on the stairs."

The employees hurried away. The four men remaining stared dumbly at the door. There was simply no way to free it: it had been designed specifically to prevent that possibility.

It was left to the locksmiths to state the obvious. "There's only one answer. We can't go through the door, so we'll have to go around it. We'll have to drill a hole in the wall."

They looked expectantly at Guenet. He was thinking of the cost, the noise, the inconvenience and the disruption of business. "No alternative?" he said.

"No alternative."

Guenet sighed. "Go through the wall."

Bigou went upstairs and came back with a set of blueprints of the vault. The men from Fichet-Bauche studied the plans for a few moments, then one of them drew a black cross to the right of the door where the wall was thinnest.

At 9:30 they switched on the electric drill.

It was a long job.

First they drilled seven or eight small holes, a few centimeters apart. Then they used a hammer and chisel to chip away at the concrete between the holes. The area at the foot of the staircase rapidly filled up with dust, and the floor was covered with chips of concrete. The two locksmiths became dirty, sweaty, exhausted and fed up.

It was enough to discourage the most determined bank robber.

At 12:00 they put down their tools. The hole was now eight inches across. The next stage was to enlarge the space until it was big enough for a man to crawl through—but first, they would have a look.

Guenet had come down to see how they were getting on.

The locksmith put his face to the hole and peered in.

"Putain de merde," he said softly.

This is a *particularly* vile French obscenity.

He turned away from the hole in the wall and looked at Guenet.

"You've been robbed," he said.

The temperature was eighty-six degrees, and rising. Jacques Guenet, the former rugby player with the impressive physique and the reassuring manner, stood at the hole in the wall, shaking in his shoes. "It's not true," he said stupidly. He said it twice.

The vault was a shambles. The floor was carpeted

with checks, bonds and stock certificates. Articles of jewelry were scattered around as if discarded: a bracelet, a necklace, a chased goblet. A pair of gas cylinders lay among the debris.

The two locksmiths stared at the stupefied bank manager. He seemed incapable of rational thought. One of them touched his shoulder and spoke to him gently, to bring him out of his state of shock. "Pull yourself together. You must call the police."

Guenet turned around. "No one must know about this!" he said fiercely. In his blind panic he clutched at the faint hope that possibly—just possibly—the intruders had merely messed up the vault without actually stealing anything.

The others knew better.

"You *must* call the police," the locksmith repeated.

Guenet nodded dumbly as reason began to return. He walked up the stairs and went to his office without speaking to anyone, ignoring the people who asked him what had happened. He sat down heavily, picked up the phone, and dialed the police station one hundred fifty yards away in the Avenue du Maréchal Foch.

The call was answered by Commissaire Albertin.

Guenet told him: "This is the Société Générale. We've been robbed."

"Don't touch anything," Albertin said. "We're on our way."

Prologue

JACQUES ALBERTIN looked more like a young executive than a detective. Aged thirty-five, he was tall, slim and bespectacled. He dressed smartly and had his hair cut short with a razor-sharp part on the left side.

By the time he arrived, accompanied by two junior detectives, the men from Fichet-Bauche had enlarged the hole to a width of eighteen inches.

Guenet explained that the vault door had been found to be jammed that morning, and the locksmiths had been unable to open it so had made the hole in the wall.

Albertin peered through the hole for a moment, then turned to his assistants. "Lecocq, you're the thinnest," he said. "See if you can get through the hole."

Inspector Lecocq put his head into the hole cautiously. He got his shoulders in, and wriggled. Halfway through, he stopped: his trousers were snagged on the rough concrete. He hesitated, then heaved. There was a tearing sound.

With a sigh of resignation he unfastened his trousers and squirmed through, leaving them behind.

It occurred to him that the thieves might still be in the vault, so he drew his revolver from his shoulder holster.

The first thing he noticed was the smell: a nauseating mixture of fumes, burning rubber and human excrement.

Then he saw the tools: drills, hammers, blowtorches, gas cylinders, gloves and face masks. On the floor were rings, silverware, an uncancelled check for fifty thousand francs ($10,325), a fat bundle of five hundred-franc notes, personal letters, stock certificates and contracts.

The debris on the scorched linoleum floor was worth close to $1.75 million.

And that was what the thieves had left behind.

Lecocq moved through the vault with his revolver in his hand. He rounded an overturned safe, clambered over a steel table and reached the far side of the underground chamber.

He breathed a sigh of relief. He was alone.

One of the safes lining the wall had been pushed forward. Lecocq looked behind it. He saw a mound of gravel and rubble, a hole a yard wide in the wall, and a tunnel that seemed to go on forever.

Now he knew how they had got in.

He turned away and something caught his eye. He looked closer: it was a beautifully engraved silver bowl of shit. He felt like throwing up.

The moment passed and he returned to the vault entrance. He put his face to the hole. Outside, Commissaire Albertin and Monsieur Guenet were growing impatient.

"What a mess," Lecocq said. "They came in through a tunnel on the Rue Gustave Deloye side."

"The sewers," Albertin said. "They must have used

the sewers." He thought for a moment. "Stay there," he told Lecocq. "I'll send a couple of men to try to get in from the street."

ON THE corner of the Rue de l'Hôtel des Postes and the Rue Gustave Deloye, across the street from the cycle stand used by the employees of the bank, two policemen pulled up a heavy manhole cover and went down into the sewer.

At the foot of the steel access ladder they stepped into the water and began to walk north, beneath the Rue Gustave Deloye. Three yards from the manhole their flashlights illuminated the entrance to the thieves' tunnel.

Someone had done an expert job. The roof of the tunnel was supported by wooden pitprops reinforced with steel. The walls had been neatly cemented. The floor was covered with a rope carpet.

Bending over, the two policemen entered the tunnel. They noticed an electric cable snaked along the carpet, and one of them stumbled over an oxyacetylene torch with its gas cylinder still attached.

Eight yards along the tunnel they emerged into the vault of the bank, to see Inspector Lecocq waiting for them, a distinctly ridiculous sight in his shirt, underpants, socks and shoes, with his gun in his hand.

THE BANK no longer belonged to Jacques Guenet. That afternoon, the police took it over.

Albertin and his men, who had answered the call, were joined by Commissaire Tholance and the Crime Squad, plus Commissaire Principal Duma and the staff of the Sûreté Urbaine. Leading the operation was Commissaire Principal Claude Besson, an insignificant-looking man in his late forties who was famous for a brilliant tax-evasion inquiry which had resulted in the jailing of nine crooked lawyers.

His first move was to have everything photographed. The police photographer, Inspector Jacob, began snapping away with his Rolleiflex. The overweight, moustached Jacob bore a remarkable resemblance to the French television cop Commissaire Bourrel, and he was forever being teased about it.

Next, the evidence was collected.

There was a ton of it.

In the vault and in the sewer the police found the following:

- 40 oxygen cylinders
- 3 oxyacetylene torches
- 10 pairs of pincers
- 2 inflatable dinghies
- 1 industrial smoke extractor with several dozen yards of flexible hose
- 20 jimmies
- waterproof overalls of the type used by sewer workers
- rubber boots, gloves and raincoats
- Margnat-Village wine bottles

bottles of Volvic mineral water
welders' goggles
a quantity of food
1 portable gas ring of the kind used for camping
1 spare canister of gas for the gas ring
several boxes of cigars

One team of policemen listed the items while another put everything into plastic bags. It was a revolting job, for a large number of men had occupied the vault for a whole weekend without sanitary facilities, and they had the unpleasant habits of thieves everywhere. The policemen cleaning up called themselves the Shit Detail. They took frequent breaks for fresh air.

Thirty-five large plastic bags were filled with the thieves' tools plus the scattered papers and the jewelry they had discarded.

The open safe-deposit boxes had revealed some curious secrets.

There was a collection of pornographic photographs, somewhat amateurish, showing naked men and women making love in couples and in groups. The people in the pictures included several well-known members of Nice's high society. One of the thieves had taped a few of the photographs to the wall.

Even more curious was a bag containing odds and ends of food: cans of soup, four pounds of sugar, some biscuits and a bar of chocolate. Why would anyone keep such things in a safe-deposit box? A bank employee explained: "There are many retired people in Nice, and they hide their secrets in our safe-deposit boxes. Some of them come here in the afternoon to eat forbidden candy or smoke a cigarette. Cans of soup? These people remember the war, and food shortages. There's a man who comes here to write his memoirs. He takes them out in the morning, works at it all day, and in the evening he puts them back in the safe. If people want to use our facilities for such eccentric purposes, who are we to say no?"

A young detective called respectfully to Commissaire Principal Besson. "Look, sir—they left a message."

Seven words were scrawled on the wall in large, bold letters: *"Sans armes, sans haine, et sans violence."* No guns, no hatred and no violence. Next to the message was drawn a Celtic cross, the symbol of a banned right-wing extremist organization called "Occident."

Besson made a note and Jacob took a picture.

The mystery of the jammed door was quickly solved: the thieves had welded it shut from the inside, presumably to guard against the faint possibility that someone might enter the vault legitimately over the weekend.

More discoveries were being made in the sewers. A blind-ended tunnel under the Rue de l'Hôtel des Postes had been used as a dump for excavated earth and rubble. The white electric cable, strung from hooks in the roof of the sewer, ran along three hundred yards of drain, through a "siphon room" (used by the town council to measure rainfall) and into an underground parking lot beneath the Place Massena —where it was plugged into an ordinary electric light socket. The power for the thieves' electric drills and other tools had been supplied free by the city.

Other police followed the trail of discarded rubber boots, blowtorches, soldering irons and assorted tunneling implements along the sewers beneath the Rue Gustave Deloye, the Rue St. Michel, left into the Rue Gioffredo and right again below the Rue Chauvain to the junction with the Rue Félix Faure. Below Rue Félix Faure they found not an ordinary drain but a wide underground road.

Nice has a large river, the Paillon, which is almost dry in summer but in winter runs through four wide underground tunnels beneath the city to the sea. The tunnels are flanked by two underground roads used for inspection of the sewers. The roads are wide enough for two cars to pass side by side. The team that robbed the Société Générale had reached the sewers via one of these roads.

One policeman followed the road north for more than a mile to the place where it surfaces behind the exhibition hall. There, in the sand of the dried-up riverbed, he found the tire tracks of a Land-Rover.

The picture was rapidly becoming clearer.

BACK IN the vault a preliminary assessment of the value of the thieves' haul was being made by Jacques Guenet, Pierre Bigou and Commissaire Principal Claude Besson.

The vault consisted of three rooms. In the largest, the safe-deposit room, three hundred and seventeen of the four thousand boxes had been broken open. The bank's treasury, an adjacent room reached by yet another steel door, had also been broken into, and the bank's entire reserves of gold ingots and cash money had been taken. The third, smallest room was the night safe, in which local stores could deposit their takings after the bank closed. (The money, bagged in special containers, was pushed through a flap in the wall at street level and fell through a shaft into the room.) From here the thieves took the weekend takings of the town's largest department store and its supermarket.

They were guessing, but they reckoned about sixty million francs.

Nearly twelve and one-half million dollars.

It was the biggest bank raid of all time.

CLAUDE BESSON, the insignificant-looking detective with a nose for financial fraud, was not easily impressed. Smart lawyers with well-known clients did not impress him any more than pickpockets and dope dealers. Criminals might be smart, but he was smarter.

Claude Besson was impressed.

The heist had been planned like a military operation. The tools, the electricity supply, the way they had used the underground road . . . Jesus Christ, they had even had an industrial smoke extractor down there! And food, and wine . . . It was as carefully prepared and efficiently executed as the most complex financial crimes he had unraveled.

There must have been ten men, perhaps twenty . . . a mass of equipment . . . months of preparation . . . days of tunneling . . . a lot of noise . . .

Yet nobody had seen anything, nobody had heard sounds, nobody had whispered rumors of an impending robbery.

The man behind the heist must be utterly brilliant: a thinker, a leader, an administrator, a brain.

He was careful, too: the day's inquiries had revealed not a single clue to his identity.

This, then, was the man Claude Besson was up against. This was his adversary.

What the hell kind of man could he be?

The Man Behind the Heist

1

I welcome all signs that a more manly, a warlike, age is about to begin, an age which, above all, will give honor to valour once again.

—Friedrich Nietzsche, Spaggiari's favorite philosopher

ALBERT SPAGGIARI was born in the village of Laragne, in the French Alps, in 1932. His father died when he was two-and-a-half years old.

His mother, a resourceful and independent woman, moved to Hyères, near the port of Toulon, taking little Albert with her. She opened a little lingerie shop and called it Caprice des Dames. The business was successful, but despite her financial independence, she married again.

Albert hated his stepfather.

At first he attended the local Anatole France primary school, but he would not settle down, so his stepfather sent him to the St. Joseph Institute, a private prep school. He was no happier there.

He was twelve years old the first time he ran away.

When the police brought him home, his mother wrote to the head teacher: "Bert is a very affectionate child; honest, courageous, loyal and good. He's not a ruffian, but he *is* very impulsive."

At fifteen he went to the Jean Aicard high school. His work was only average, but he developed a passion for literature. His two particular interests were adventure stories and political essays. He had an unusually lively imagination. He had an air rifle, and although he would never shoot birds, he used to fire at old tin cans and make believe they were people.

He became obsessed with Salvatore Giuliano, a Sicilian bandit and romantic popular hero of the late nineteen-forties. He devoured everything written about Giuliano, and fantasized about meeting the man. At the age of sixteen he ran away from home again, headed for Italy.

He took a roundabout route, going by boat to Tunisia, traveling along the North African coast, then catching another boat to Sicily. He never got past the Italian immigration control. After spending several days in jail he was returned to his stepfather, covered with lice.

The note he had left on the kitchen table foreshadowed his future political ideas: *"La cause en vaut les moyens."* The end justifies the means.

Many adolescent boys are unruly and dream of adventure: maturity generally brings their dreams down to earth and tempers their character with self-discipline. Albert Spaggiari was different: in a way, he never grew up.

In 1950, when he was eighteen, he joined the army and volunteered for the Indochina Expeditionary Force. The French had not yet been thrown out of Vietnam, and the Americans had not arrived.

Asia was good for Spaggiari. He liked to travel, his thirst for adventure was slaked, and he began to develop his political ideas in the kind of colonialist environment which nourished right-wing extremism. He was assigned to the Third Battalion parachute corps.

He was a useful soldier, winning three decorations, but he was very bad at taking orders from other people, and this fault excluded him from promotion: he never got higher than corporal.

In 1954 he was convicted of theft and sentenced to four years' imprisonment. He had been at a Saigon brothel with a number of fellow soldiers, and a row had broken out with the madam. The other soldiers left, but Spaggiari stayed behind and robbed the till. His comrades claimed they had been cheated, and Spaggiari had merely taken back money that was rightfully theirs; but the military court was not impressed by this defense.

It was also the year of the Battle of Dienbienphu, one of the greatest disasters in French military history, when twenty thousand crack troops were defeated by an army of peasant farmers. But Spaggiari was not there: he was in chains aboard the *Pasteur,* on his way home.

With remission he was out of jail in 1957 and he went to live quietly with his mother back in Hyères, over the shop. There he met Marcelle Audi, a young nurse, and married her.

Audi—he always called her by her surname—was a small, plain woman with brown hair and dark eyes. She was very much the typical nurse, with a brisk walk and precise, rapid movements. Her clothes were simple but well-chosen, and she had a strong character and a certain winning charm. Unlike her husband she was somewhat guarded, introverted; an observer rather than a doer.

The couple were not passionately in love, but were enormously good friends, loyal rather than faithful to one another, and—importantly—sharing the same political and philosophical ideas. Audi was an emotional anchor in Spaggiari's stormy life, and while his fortunes were to be uneven, she would always be able to earn a living as a nurse.

For a while it seemed Spaggiari might be settling down. In reality the quiet country air was choking him. The call of adventure became irresistible, and one spring morning he and his wife caught a boat to Dakar, in the French African colony of Senegal.

There he worked as a coppersmith and Audi as a

nurse. They planned to make their fortune. It did not work out. By 1960 they were back in France.

They moved to Nice, and lived on the Route de Marseilles in the working-class quarter. In France a nurse can have her own practice, giving first-aid treatment and injections; and this Audi did. Spaggiari tried his luck in real estate, without conspicuous success.

This was the time of the "wind of change" in Africa, when European countries were disengaging themselves from their colonies with varying degrees of difficulty. French Algeria suffered a brutal internecine war as Algerian-born whites fought against dispossession. Spaggiari joined the Organisation Armée Secrete, an illegal movement in support of the white Algerians. Like the IRA, the OAS embraced people of more or less militant outlook and varied politics (though they were all right-wing). Groups within it included Catena which assisted fugitives to escape from the police, and Commando Delta which carried out assassinations and fund-raising bank raids. In later years, when the liberation of Algeria was a *fait accompli,* OAS lost its *raison d'être;* but it remained an umbrella for right-wing extremists and neo-Nazis.

Spaggiari wanted to be part of Commando Delta, the special operations squad, but it seems that the leaders believed him too unsuitable to be trusted—a snub which was to be repeated more than once in his career.

General Charles de Gaulle was hated by the OAS. A

right-winger, he had at one time been openly *sympathisant de l'Algérie Française,* but when he became president reality took over. He dropped Algeria like a hot brick, and the OAS felt bitterly betrayed.

In 1961 Spaggiari went to Spain and had a clandestine meeting at a Madrid swimming pool with Pierre Lagaillarde, former leader of the right-wing Algerian students. Spaggiari told him: "I am at your disposal. I will carry out any operation you see fit to order."

In November of that year Spaggiari had his big chance. The reviled President de Gaulle was to visit Hyères, and his motorcade would pass the Caprice des Dames lingerie shop. Spaggiari wrote to Lagaillarde. He sent the letter by registered post, mailing it at Vintimille and signing a false name. The message was melodramatic: "Lieutenant Lagaillarde, I await from you only one order—the execution order."

Spaggiari arrived in Hyères from Nice on the morning of November 8, 1961. The shops were all closed and shuttered for the presidential visit. He secreted the key to his mother's shop, parked a getaway motorcycle in the back yard, and went into the empty apartment on the first floor. He had a Mauser rifle.

At around four o'clock the motorcade entered the appropriately named Avenue Charles de Gaulle. Despite the bad weather the president was standing up in his limousine, smiling and waving to the cheering crowds. At 4:12 P.M. de Gaulle was in Spaggiari's sights, less than five yards away—an easy target for the man who had been a crack shot among the paratroopers of the elite Third Battalion.

Spaggiari did not pull the trigger, of course. Lagaillarde never sent the execution order—like other OAS leaders he did not take the theatrical Albert Spaggiari seriously—and for once in his life Spaggiari accepted authority.

In March 1962, police raided a villa in Villefranche sur Mer, an expensive resort between Nice and Cap Ferrat. They found an illegal printing press used to produce OAS leaflets, and an arms cache. A small group of extremists was arrested, and Spaggiari was one of them.

The court of the Alpes Maritimes *département* (state) sentenced him to four years in the St. Martin prison at Ré. His comrades got probation. It is not clear why Spaggiari was singled out for special treatment, but the likelihood is that the authorities knew about his abortive attempt to assassinate de Gaulle.

He was freed in 1966 and returned to his wife and friends in Nice. He got interested in photography, and opened a shop at 56 Route de Marseilles, called Photo La Vallière.

Spaggiari spent his evenings in bistros and bars, talking to OAS friends or old comrades from Vietnam. He joined another right-wing organization, the bizarre SS Weapons Brotherhood.

During this period he made a mysterious trip to

Munich, center of German neo-Nazism. Audi told people he had gone to learn German with the intention of becoming a professional translator. This unlikely story was never borne out by events: at no time did he attempt to get a job as interpreter, and he did not become fluent in German.

This part of his life story is notably vague. He seems to have increased his contacts with right-wing organizations all over Europe, and he may have had dealings with the CIA. He was in touch with the Italian neo-Fascists, and he is suspected of being involved in arms smuggling. In 1969, when Russian tanks rolled through the streets of Prague, Spaggiari was in Czechoslovakia with false identity papers and a forged press card. He was vague about the trip: "We ought to do something for our friends," he said. "We should help the patriotic Czechs."

He showed some talent as a photographer. He went to North Africa and spent some time in the Sahara Desert, living with the nomads and taking photographs. Photography gave him an entrée into a rather higher stratum of Nice society, and he became a semiofficial photographer for the town. (It is an exaggeration to say—as some Niçoises do—that the town is run by the OAS; but there is no doubt that Spaggiari was not the only person to be accepted both in official circles and among the right-wing extremists.) Eating and drinking with a wealthier set, he secured his position by becoming a big spender, and his tips were legendary for their generosity.

In 1972 he bought a ruined farmhouse in the forest of Bézaudun not far from Nice. He paid very little for it, but with the help of a local builder he transformed the place. He worked on it for months, putting in new windows, retiling the roof, adding balconies and installing modern heating. He used stone and wood and the local red brick, giving the house a natural, earthy look.

He and Audi became very attached to the place. They hung weapons on the walls—although Spaggiari never used them: he would not even shoot the rabbits that ruined his vegetable patch, and if Audi wanted to kill a chicken for dinner she had to take it to the village butcher. Also on the wall were a huge photograph of Hitler and an SS emblem.

When he drove up in his Land-Rover and parked by the hundred-year-old oak tree, his Doberman pinschers Packa and Vesta would run out to greet him, jump into the vehicle and lick his hands. In the evenings he would sit by the fire and read. His library was extensive: Balzac, Zola, Flaubert . . . and, of course, Nietzsche.

Eventually he rented the photography shop to his manager and moved out to Bézaudun permanently. Audi set up yet another nursing practice, and Albert raised chickens.

Again it looked as if he might be settling down; but once again, appearances were deceptive.

An acquaintance of his, twenty-eight-year-old Gérard Rang, was being watched by the police in 1974. The blond, stocky Rang was owner of the notorious Chi-Chi nightclub in Haut de Cagnes, where the stage show featured live group sex. Rang, who was to figure largely in the heist of the century, came under suspicion in 1974 in a police investigation into forged checks. Rang—if it were he—was not just forging *signatures,* but actually printing checkbooks. One of the books was found in a sewer grating at his club. It occurred to the police that Spaggiari, one of Rang's right-wing comrades, had all the facilities for photo-printing the checks at his photography shop. However, they failed to collect sufficient evidence to bring a prosecution.

It was also in 1974 that Spaggiari rented a safe-deposit box in the vault of the Société Générale bank in the Avenue Jean Médecin.

RESTLESS, UNDISCIPLINED, adventurous, obsessive: what makes a man this way?

One of his close friends had this to say: "It might have been different if he had become a father. It would have matured him, calmed him down. But it never happened."

Audi was unable to bear children. The couple tried to adopt, but as a known member of an illegal organization Albert was disqualified from adoption. Even without his OAS background, his prison record might well have been viewed with disfavor by the adoption authorities.

He certainly wanted a child. He himself said: "I tried everything, but a member of the OAS is not allowed to adopt."

But the key to Spaggiari's character lies farther in the past.

*Layman fondly imagine that babies are oblivious to tragedy. The reverse is true. A trauma in the first few years of life may explain much about a person's eventual character. Albert Spaggiari's father died when he was two and a half years old.

To a child, a father represents both discipline and love; and through this combination of apparently contradictory characteristics the child learns the concept of benign authority. The father also provides an image with which the son can identify, and gives him a pattern to follow.

Of course, not every fatherless child is permanently scarred by the trauma. The place of the dead man may be taken by an uncle, a friend of the family, or a stepfather.

But for some reason Albert rejected his stepfather. Therefore, the father figure in his life represented authority *without* love.

This may be responsible for several features of Spaggiari's personality.

*The authors are indebted to José von Buehler for assistance with this passage.

His interest in weapons, the SS and political militancy may represent an obsession with tyrannical (loveless) authority.

His love of adventure stories, his juvenile identification with the bandit Salvatore Giuliano, and his photographs of Hitler may be seen as a search for a father figure.

The shiftless, up-and-down pattern of his life—traveling, changing jobs, never settling down—may be due to the lack of a father to imitate.

But most importantly, his rebelliousness and his criminality are a rejection of the authority he never learned to love.

He has spent his life proving that he knows better than his stepfather.

Spaggiari Makes his Plans

2

Non, je ne regrette rien.
—Albert Spaggiari

NICE is a lot like Bournemouth, only better.

Founded in about 350 B.C. by a tribe of Greek sailors, it remained a fishing village until the nineteenth century when wealthy English holidaymakers invented the French Riviera. In 1822 the growing colony of idle English built themselves a two-and-one-half-mile long promenade, the town's most distinctive feature, now called the Promenade des Anglais.

Situated on the Baie des Anges, twenty miles from the Italian border, it is the leading resort town of the Côte d'Azur. It is sheltered by low hills to the north, and it rains only sixty times in the average year. There is an airport, a university, and several art museums. The population is about three hundred fifty thousand.

The Paillon River divides the east side, with the harbor, commercial district and winding streets of the Old Town, from the west side, consisting of newer property and the airport.

Like Bournemouth, it has a large resident population of elderly and retired people; and it is this feature that most interests a bank like the Société Générale. One of the larger French banks, its main Nice branch is designed to appeal to the elderly. The imposing white stone façade occupies a whole city block, and its vaguely Italianate architecture apes that of the Palais de Justice, the town's courthouse. Inside the bank, the main hall has an enormously high ceiling supported by marbled pillars. The arched windows are protected by wrought iron grilles, very different from the plate glass shop windows of more modern banks.

After the heist of the century the bank understandably saw the need for a more modern image, and today part of the main hall is a huge open-plan office, with contemporary furniture and decorated in orange and white, aluminum and glass. But when Albert Spaggiari first entered its doors in September 1974 it retained the soothing atmosphere of a traditional solicitor's office.

This was particularly noticeable in the vault—much used by those wealthy retired people, who often prefer to keep their riches in the tangible forms of gold and jewelry. There was an old couch, some steel chairs and tables, and several large pairs of scissors chained to the tables in the old-fashioned manner. The floor was covered with brown linoleum, and the cabinets containing the safe-deposit boxes had the same dated look as the bank's façade.

There were seven armored cabinets, containing a total of around four thousand boxes. The boxes were of two sizes: some twelve inches by eight inches and stretching two feet back; others twenty-four inches by sixteen inches and the same depth. There were two keys to each box, and both had to be used to unlock the box. One was kept by the customer, the other by the bank.

The cabinets were opened every morning. When a customer wanted to go to his box, he first had to sign the vault log. Then a guard would escort him to his box. The customer would insert his key, the guard would insert the bank's key, and the box would open. After that the guard would leave the customer alone. The customer could stay as long as he liked. When he had completed what he came to do, he would close the box and it would lock automatically. At the end of the day the cabinets would be closed and locked, then the guard would close the twenty-ton vault door.

Two years later Spaggiari was to tell the Examining Magistrate: "I got the idea to break in the very day I rented a safe-deposit box at the Société Générale in

September 1974. It developed in my mind, bit by bit, until the moment when I realized it really *could* be done."

However, Spaggiari told many lies during that interrogation. "Every time I went down to my safe-deposit box I learned a little more about the vault. I paced out the size of the room. I made little drawings. I even took photographs—nobody seemed to mind."

But how, he was asked, did he know that there was no alarm system? "I bought an alarm clock with a very loud ring. I set it for 1:00 A.M., then put it in my safe-deposit box late one afternoon. At 1:00 A.M. I was sitting outside the Taverne Alsacienne, across the street from the bank. I stayed there until 2:00 A.M. Nothing happened. The next day I opened the box. The clock was there, still ticking, but the alarm had wound itself down."

It is possible that a sensitive modern alarm system might have been set off by the noise of an alarm clock; but it is unlikely that a planner as careful as Spaggiari would have relied on such a dubious method of checking. In any event, both this story and the tale about pacing the vault and taking photographs were quickly discounted by the police. For the vault log—signed by each customer every time he enters—revealed that Spaggiari had been there only twice: once when he first rented the box, and a second time in January 1975.

When this was pointed out he came up with another

story. "There is a branch of the Société Générale at 52 Route de Marseilles, next door but one to my shop. I had an account there, and the cashier was a customer at the shop. We were neighbors, we both owned houses in the street, and he was garrulous. He had worked at the main branch in the Avenue Jean Médecin, and as a cashier he had access to the vault. Bit by bit I got from him the details of the layout, without his realizing what I was up to. And it was he who told me that there was no alarm system."

Spaggiari named the cashier. He had recently died.

The story might be true, but a loose-tongued banker is a rarity, and it would have been a remarkable piece of good fortune for a villain to find one on his doorstep. How Spaggiari got this preliminary information must therefore remain an open question, with the balance of probability in favor of an inside informant who may never be identified.

Spaggiari also needed to know the weight of the steel cabinets. He claimed he simply asked the guard. The answer he got was thirty tons, and he allowed in his plans for double that. This story is probably true, for it would account for his second visit to the vault in January 1975.

There is, however, no mystery about how he obtained plans of the drain system around the bank. Blueprints of the town's entire sewage system are available to any member of the public at the town hall. Spaggiari introduced himself as a discotheque promoter and said he wanted to build a club in an underground location. The officials of the public works department were most helpful, and gave him a copy of blueprint number 16, drawn to the scale of 1:1,000—a large, clear map.

From the blueprint Spaggiari was able to figure out the shortest route from the bank to the underground road beside the Paillon tunnel. He then checked the route on foot. His own account of this period is basically credible, if highly colored: "I spent six nights in a row in the sewers, wading through the filth with the rats and the smell. I explored the system step by step until I knew every corner, every dead end. Whenever I got lost I would simply climb up a shaft, lift the manhole, and look around the street until I got my bearings again."

It may not have taken six nights, but he would hardly have been so foolish as to poke his head up into the street; but his explanation established a number of vital points:

1. It was possible to drive from the Avenue Marechal Lyautey down a purpose-built ramp on to the dried-up bed of the Paillon River and from there—having removed a flimsy corrugated-iron barrier a foot or two high—straight down the underground road.

2. The point at which the road passed most closely to the bank was beneath the junction of the Rue Félix Faure and the Rue Chauvain.

3. A second entrance to the underground road—

admitting people, but not cars—was available at the Place Massena at the top of the Rue Félix Faure. Here there was an underground parking lot leading to a "siphon room," which town council employees could enter to check the level of rainfall. The parking lot was guarded with closed-circuit television, and one of the cameras pointed directly at the door to the siphon room; but the camera's view could be effectively blocked simply by parking a car between it and the door. Using this entrance when possible would save a two-mile drive. Here, too, Spaggiari could remove an electric light and plug in the cable for his lights and power tools.

4. There was a third entrance, much closer to the bank but also more dangerous: the manhole at the corner of Rue de l'Hôtel des Postes and Rue Gustave Deloye. The heaviest items of equipment, which would be difficult to transport through the sewage pipes from the underground road to the bank, could be lowered through this manhole. However, it would have to be used as little as possible.

5. Beneath the Rue de l'Hôtel des Postes, at the front of the bank, was a blind-ended drain that could be used to deposit the loose earth and rubble from the digging.

6. The tunnel from the drain through to the wall of the vault would be opened in the sewer beneath the Rue Gustave Deloye, close to the manhole.

The finer points had yet to be worked out, but the basic plan was there, and it looked highly feasible. Now Spaggiari needed the men to carry it out.

EARLY IN 1976 Spaggiari made contact with a group known as *Le Gang des Marsaillais*—the Marseilles Mob. Marseilles had long been France's criminal capital, and although the narcotics trade had moved east to Nice, Marseilles was still the place to go for felonious expertise.

The gang was interested in Spaggiari's plans, and agreed to send a team to go over the ground. However, here there was a snag: their tunneling expert, an Italian known as The Mason, was in jail. He would have to be sprung—at Spaggiari's expense. Spaggiari swallowed this somewhat dubious story and forked over $6,200, and The Mason was duly sprung from the Bourges prison.*

The team from Marseilles entered the sewer system from the Place Massena underground parking lot via the siphon room. They looked at the underground road, walked through the sewers, and saw the place where Spaggiari planned to tunnel. The Mason examined the texture of the soil. "This is pudding," he said. "The tunnel will have to be reinforced."

*The authors—and indeed, the police—know The Mason's real name; but he was never caught, and under French law he may not be identified until he is convicted or confesses to the crime. For the same reason the reader will find several criminals referred to by nicknames or simply by an initial.

They looked at the bank from the outside, and viewed the riverbed entrance to the underground road.

They liked the plan.

They did not like Spaggiari.

They turned him down.

Like the army, the OAS and Pierre Lagaillarde, the Marseilles Mob saw something in Spaggiari they mistrusted: a hint of unreality, a touch of megalomania, an obsessive, unstable personality.

They gave him back his rubber boots and disappeared. Only The Mason remained, perhaps out of a sense of indebtedness; so Spaggiari got some return for his $6,200 investment.

However, Spaggiari now had to put together a team. It was his most difficult problem and in the end his choice of collaborators was the ultimate flaw in the operation.

The way he recruited Francis Pellegrin was typical.

In the Rue Félix Faure was a café also called the Félix Faure. In 1976 it was Nice's most fashionable meeting place. The barman made excellent champagne cocktails, and served several brands of American bourbon. The food was good, and the clientele young, attractive and beautifully dressed. The cars were double-parked outside (double-parking is *de rigueur* for the trendy Niçois) and the pavement was blocked by motorcycles. (In the Riviera bikes are not the prerogative of Hell's Angels, and in the mild climate you don't have to dress like a mountaineer to ride one.) It was at this chic waterhole that Spaggiari met Pellegrin.

Pellegrin was a small-time crook, what the French call a *demi sel.* Nearsighted, ungraceful, his face pitted by acne, there was nothing appealing about him. Nor was he clever. Not to put too fine a point on it, he was downright stupid.

He had recently arrived from his small-town home of Beaulieu without a centime in his pocket. Spaggiari awed him. Spaggiari seemed elegant, cool, a mad genius with a lot of class. He could hardly believe that Albert was a chicken farmer. "Goebbels raised chickens too, you know," Spaggiari told him. Pellegrin did not know whether he was having his leg pulled or not.

The *demi sel* was uneasy with Spaggiari, and felt inferior; but to his surprise Albert took him to one side one evening and said: "I know I can rely on your discretion. I have to make some good contacts very fast. If you can help me, I'll see you don't regret it."

Most of the team was recruited this way. There were four exceptions: G—— and P—— were white Algerians and OAS comrades; Captain V—— was a Vietnam veteran; and The Mason came from the Marseilles Mob. Another nineteen villains were contacted by means of the underworld grapevine: Pellegrin met someone who knew a driver; Spaggiari had a friend who knew people looking for a way to make a fast buck; and so on.

And here is the first of several mysteries surrounding the police handling of this case. Any halfway competent detective force has its informers among the local villianry: men who are basically criminals, and accepted as such by other criminals, but who are not averse to making a little extra money by passing tips to the police. English detectives call them snouts; the French call them *indics.* Now, intelligent and successful professional criminals keep their plans secret, for they know very well that they cannot trust anyone but their close associates. But Spaggiari was *actively publicizing* his need for men in every *louche* (seedy) bar in town. It is very hard to believe that not one of the Nice *indics* got to hear of the impending job. Nevertheless, no one in the Nice police had any idea that Spaggiari was planning something. This kind of apparent incompetence occurs more than once in the story of the heist of the century, and it is a theme to which we will return.

Spaggiari's next task was to acquire the equipment needed, and he did this with his usual scrupulous caution.

For carrying the tools he bought several bags made of heavy-duty canvas of the type used on yachts. Those came from the Rinascente department store in Milan.

Ten pairs of Swedish-steel scissors, made in Stockholm, were bought for cash in Belgium.

He bought twenty small hammers, twelve large hammers, and several bricklayers' trowels; thirty assorted chisels of various sizes, a roll of plastic bags, six charges of dynamite and three oxyacetylene torches.

Thirty flashlights, all Super-Limijet brand, were acquired in various shops in Nice's Old Town and at the Cap 3000 department store in Villeneuve Loubet. They were bought singly, for the most part; and Spaggiari was furious when he discovered that one of his *demi sels* had bought three in one shop.

He bought a wheelbarrow and several buckets for removing the earth excavated in the tunnel; wooden boards and beams for supporting the roof of the tunnel; and a number of one hundred-and-ten pound bags of cement for the walls.

Three hundred meters of electric cable were purchased in lengths of forty and fifty yards in shops in Nice, Menton and Antibes.

He bought two AEG electric drills, a heavy-duty hydraulic lever, and a small laser costing over two thousand dollars that would cut through four inches of reinforced concrete per minute.

He bought a first-aid kit of considerable sophistication, a portable stove, cylinders of fuel for the oxyacetylene torches, rubber boots and waterproof overalls of the type used by sewer workers, and scores of pairs of gloves ranging from protective gauntlets to surgical gloves.

He bought an industrial smoke extractor to keep the air in the tunnel breathable.

Almost the only items stolen were several dozen

heavy staples hammered into the roof of the drain to carry the electric cable high above the water level. These came from a building site in Grasse. No doubt some petty criminal instructed to buy the hooks could not resist the temptation to steal them and pocket the money given him by Spaggiari.

For transporting all the equipment along several hundred yards of drain, Spaggiari got two inflatable rubber dinghies and a number of inner tubes for truck tires.

Spades, shovels, screwdrivers, goggles, crowbars . . . the list seems endless. They were bought all over Western Europe: never conspicuously, always in small numbers, and frequently in large department stores. Spaggiari intended that the equipment his team left behind them after the heist would give the police a lot of work to absolutely no result; and this is exactly what happened.

Spaggiari now needed somewhere to keep all this equipment, so he borrowed a villa at Castagniers, a village a few miles out of Nice. He could have stored everything at his farm, but he decided the villa would be safer.

This was a very bad mistake.

A Jealous Wife

3

The ear of jealousy heareth all things.
—The Wisdom of Solomon

THE DETECTION of The Sewer Rats—as Spaggiari's team came to be called—actually began ten days before the robbery; and it began with The Case of the Jealous Wife.

The woman was the wife of a fun-loving middle-aged businessman who owned a trucking company. He had salt-and-pepper hair and a trim body: he was attractive for his age, and he knew it only too well. He enjoyed practical jokes and liked to show off his physique on the beach at Villeneuve Loubet. The business was successful, and the couple had a twenty-year-old son.

A Jealous Wife

Early in 1976 the woman—let us call her Madame V———discovered that her husband had set up a mistress in a villa at Cagnes sur Mer. She was furious, and talked to a lawyer about divorce, but in the end she decided to do nothing, say nothing, and wait for the affair to end.

On July 8, 1976 Monsieur V—— went to Lyons on business. That evening the wife discovered that a key was missing. It was the key to a villa in Castagniers that belonged not to Monsieur V—— but to a friend of his. The friend lived some distance away, and the couple had agreed to keep an eye on it for him, to air the place occasionally and make it look occupied so that burglars would be discouraged. Now Madame V—— suspected that her husband had not gone to Lyons on business, but had taken another little nymphet to the villa in Castagniers.

The next day, July 9, Madame V—— got out her cream-colored Peugeot and drove toward Castagniers. She had no specific plans as she drove at a steady fifty miles per hour past the construction site for the new *Nice-Matin* skyscraper, past the Azur gas station and the fashionable Servelle Restaurant. She was chain-smoking, and her forty-year-old face was lined with strain.

The villa was a short distance from the main road, but in a quiet area. Built in the style of a Provençal farmhouse, it was surrounded by olive trees, and had a red-tiled roof and rough-cast eggshell colored walls.

It was set high on a hillside, and had a breathtaking view.

Madame V—— stopped the car some distance away. She could see that the shutters were open. The villa was occupied.

She hesitated for a moment, then turned the car in a fast circle and drove away at top speed. She had seen enough: she was firmly convinced that her husband was being unfaithful to her again, but she did not have the nerve to knock on the door and catch him red-handed.

She went home and tried not to cry.

She had confused motives for what she did next. She wanted to be certain her husband was there, she wanted him to know she knew what he was doing, and she wanted to embarrass him. She picked up the phone and called the owner of the villa.

"Have you rented the villa?" she asked.

"No, I haven't. Why?"

"I happened to drive by a while ago and I noticed that the shutters were open. I thought I'd better check."

"No, there shouldn't be anyone there. You still have the keys, don't you?"

"Yes," she lied.

"Could your husband drive up there and check?"

"He's not here—he went to Lyons on business." There was a pause. Madame V—— went on: "I'm worried. There are so many burglaries on the Côte d'Azur, with all these hippies . . ."

That last line seemed to strike home.

"All right," said the owner. "It's my villa. I'll call the police."

FRANCE HAS two police forces. Large towns have the *Police Judiciaire,* which operates much like an English city police force and is similarly controlled by the Ministry of the Interior. The countryside and the small towns are policed by the *Gendarmerie,* a military body under the control of the Army minister. Gendarmes are always uniformed, and they have no detectives: they are obliged to report criminal matters to the nearest *Police Judiciare,* which is then responsible for investigation.

The owner of the villa at Castagniers phoned the Plan du Var brigade of gendarmes. The call was taken by Gendarme Claude Destreil, who—like all gendarmes—was a clean-cut young man with short hair and a blue khaki shirt. Like country policemen everywhere, he was interested in anything out-of-the-ordinary that happened on his territory. And, since at the time he had nothing more interesting to do than to fill out a tedious report, he collected his colleague Gendarme Patrick Gruau and drove up to the villa.

Destreil parked the small blue station wagon under an olive tree and the two men looked around. Gruau climbed the seventeen steps to the front door and knocked several times without getting an answer.

They both admired the view across the valley of the Var River.

The villa's shutters were indeed open, and so was a window. The garage was locked, but they were able to look inside and take the registration number of a brand-new metallic-gray Peugeot 504 parked inside.

There were no signs of a break-in.

The gendarmes returned to the station. That afternoon they discovered that the Peugeot was registered to a musical-instrument salesman from Béziers, two hundred miles away.

At 6:30 in the evening they returned to the villa to double-check. This time they had more luck.

There were two expensive cars in the drive—a Mercedes and a Renault 17—and four men sitting on the steps.

The gendarmes began to question them. The eldest of the four men explained: "We've rented the villa, and we're waiting for a friend to bring the keys."

The owner had said quite definitely that he had *not* rented the villa to anyone. The gendarmes asked the men for their papers, and noted down the details:

Dominique Poggi, of 23 Rue Fourmillière, Antibes, born February 16, 1926 in Farinole, Corsica;

Daniel Michelucci, of 20 Rue Samatan, Marseilles, born October 6, 1947 in Marseilles;

Christian Duche, of 36 Esplanade de la Tourette, Marseilles, born March 8, 1947 in Marseilles;

Alain Pons—no papers.

"We know the owner has not rented the villa," Destreil told them.

Poggi smiled. "Well, we haven't actually rented it," he said. "A friend of ours, Raymond, got it for us, and he is bringing the key. You can check—he has a restaurant on the beach at St. Laurent du Var."

The gendarmes were not impressed.

Poggi winked and said: "We're having a little party here tonight . . . just among ourselves . . . know what I mean?"

There were plainly no women around, and these four did not strike the gendarmes as overtly homosexual. Destreil said: "All right, let's go and see this Raymond."

Poggi hesitated. "Actually, he hasn't got the key himself. A friend has it."

"And where does the friend live?"

"Near the stadium."

"So we'll go there."

The four men shrugged and got up. The gendarmes heard the sound of a car engine. They turned and saw the roof of a car just visible over the tops of the trees. The car suddenly stopped, reversed and drove away. However, the gendarmes were able to identify it as a Renault 5.

The six men left: Destreil and Gruau in their police station wagon, Duche in the Mercedes and the other three in the Renault.

The address to which they went was that of Madame V——, who had started the whole thing because she suspected her husband of infidelity. She was at home. Her son was there with her, and she seemed to have been crying.

Now there were eight people in the living-room.

Gendarme Gruau questioned Madame V——. "Do you have the keys to the villa at Castagniers?"

"No," she replied. "My husband took them. He is being unfaithful to me with a whore in the villa."

"That's not true," Poggi interrupted. "He gave the key to Raymond, who was supposed to give it to us."

This was something of a shock for Madame V——. "But why?"

Poggi went into his nudge-nudge routine again. "We were going to have a little party . . . you know."

Destreil had heard this number before. He decided to cut things short. He turned to Madame V——'s son. "Please telephone this Monsieur Raymond and get him here quickly. Just tell him that his friends want to see him."

The young man did as he was told, and Raymond arrived fifteen minutes later. When the doorbell rang the gendarmes asked everyone to leave the room so that they could question Raymond alone and see whether his story tallied. However, they were not very experienced at this sort of thing, and Poggi caught them wrong-footed by answering the door and whispering a few words to Raymond.

It looked highly suspicious, but it was hardly an arrestable offense.

Destreil looked at Gruau and shrugged. "We blew it," he said.

THE GENDARMES went through the motions of questioning Raymond, but not surprisingly his story tallied exactly with Poggi's. The gendarmes reported the incident to Pierre Dufour, the moustached chief of the Plan du Var brigade, who shrugged and told them to keep the file open. At the end of the day the only satisfied person was Madame V——, who had learned that her husband had not been unfaithful.

Over the next few days the gendarmes took the inquiry as far as it would go. They discovered that neither of the two cars used by the four men was owned by any of them: the Mercedes was registered to Alain Benisson, of 28 Rue Massenole, Marseilles, born September 3, 1942; and the Renault 17 to Louis Belayle, of 88 Avenue Camipelletan, Marseilles, born February 18, 1951 in Marseilles. They were able to trace the Renault 5 whose roof they had seen hastily reversing away from the villa—a woman living near the villa had complained that the car had reversed all over her lawn, and she had taken the number. She could not give a description of the driver, but the gendarmes were able to establish that it was registered to André Fénouil, of 5 Rue du Chaipitre, Nimes, born December 13, 1931 in Oran, Algeria. Fénouil had a criminal record: he had served twelve years for murder.

There were only six gendarmes at the Plan du Var station: Chief Dufour, Destreil and Gruau, and Andre Diminato, Edmond Sanchez and Patrice Sloma. They were all intrigued by the mystery of the villa at Castagniers. There was no point in contacting the detectives at Nice; for no crime had been committed, and they really had no information to pass on—just vague suspicions. Besides, they found it rather exciting. It was not often that the men in the blue khaki shirts got a chance to prove they knew more than the city detectives with their made-to-measure suits and their after-shave.

The gendarmes, too, had their *indics.* One in particular was a bistro owner who did a little illegal bookmaking on the side. Over a *vichy-fraises* he told them: "Your four visitors were in here. They told me they were working on a job. A big job."

THIS WAS as far as the gendarmes got before the heist. Nevertheless, it is truly astonishing that they should have had four cars, ten names and a rumor when the Nice police—who were supposed to be the detectives—had nothing. It is as if a traffic policeman in Surbiton were to know of an impending raid on a West End bank of which Scotland Yard was totally ignorant. However, perhaps this point has been labored enough.

The incident at Castagniers jolted Spaggiari. The

villa was, of course, his headquarters, where he had stored the considerable quantity of equipment for the heist. And this brush with the forces of law and order came very shortly before zero hour. In fact, the heist had been planned originally for that very evening, and had been postponed when Spaggiari learned that Nice was to have a very important visitor that weekend.

At 5:30 p.m. on Saturday July 10, 1976, the Mystère 20 presidential jet hit the runway at Nice airport and Giscard d'Estaing got out. This is the only area of the South of France that voted for him: the other southern *départements* favored Mitterand, the loser. The president emerged from the plane in a gray suit, looking relaxed and suntanned. He waved to the crowd on the airport terrace.

He was driven along the Promenade des Anglais—thronged with supporters waving Tricolor flags—to St. Jean Cap Ferrat for a naval review. After that he returned to Nice's Palais Massena, the mayoral residence, for a reception.

He accepted flowers from two little girls in national costume, signed his name in the *livre d'or,* accepted a coral sculpture from Mayor Jacques Médecin (who was also Minister of Tourism in d'Estaing's cabinet), and shook hands with some of the six hundred invited guests.

One of the guests was a well-dressed man in a tailored alpaca suit with a cape hung loosely over his shoulders. He had a muscular build and a catlike walk. His dark face was full of character: dark eyes twinkling with ironical amusement, a few strands of gray in his brown hair; a long French nose, a strong chin, a ready smile. He seemed at ease, but watchful. He was the mayor's semi-official photographer, Albert Spaggiari, but he was not taking photographs. He was checking out the presidential security with professional interest.

Some of the guards had little red pins in their lapels; others were not identifiable superficially—Spaggiari looked twice at a woman using her powder case, and decided she was a bodyguard. Outside, on the roofs, he spotted several more.

Police reinforcements had been brought in from Cannes, Toulon and even as far as Marseilles. Nice was crawling with cops. The city was under maximum security. They were probably checking even the drains for bombs.

It was the drains that bothered Spaggiari. His plans were so close to fruition; but there had been the incident at Castagniers yesterday, and today they might be checking the drains. Dear God, he had put some work into those drains . . .

DIGGING THE tunnel from the sewer to the wall of the bank vault took most of May and June.

Every other day, the metallic-gray Peugeot 504 would enter the underground parking lot at the Place Massena around suppertime and park a couple of yards from the siphon-room door, blocking the view of the closed-circuit television camera. Then a Citroën 2CV truck would pull in behind the Peugeot, concealed from the camera and therefore unseen by the garage attendant in his booth.

The Mason and his assistants would get out of the Citroën truck, pick up their equipment, and go through the siphon room and on to the underground road. From there they would wade through the sewers, bending over—the pipes were less than three feet high—to the bank.

Two men worked at the front of the tunnel, one loosening the earth with picks and the other shoveling it away. A third man carried it the few yards to the blind-ended drain used as a dump.

The tunnel was only two feet across at the point where it opened into the sewer. Spaggiari insisted that the entrance to the tunnel had to look as if it had been made by the town's sewer workers, or by the phone company: its concrete walls had to be painted the exact color. The idea was that anyone with legitimate work to do in the sewers during the daytime would pass Spaggiari's tunnel without a second glance. For the weekend of the presidential visit the tunnel mouth was blocked with board and painted over.

As the tunnel progressed, The Mason followed behind the diggers, propping the roof of the tunnel and cementing its walls. The Mason was a professional, the son of a builder, who had found that his services attracted higher rewards from criminals than from the construction industry. He supervised this stage of the operation.

Spaggiari turned up from time to time, checking on progress and always bringing a few bottles of wine for the dusty throats of the workers. Once he asked the men to turn on the electric drills while he went topside to find out whether they could be heard from the street.

The tunneling was debilitating for the two men at the front. One night one of them passed out. There was a moment of panic: the man—G——, the youngest member of the team—began to shiver all over, and then threw up. He was carried to the siphon room, then driven home.

Thereafter Spaggiari imposed a strict regime on the tunnelers. Each team was sent down only one day in three. Before going down, they had to abstain from alcohol and coffee, and get ten hours' sleep. He gave them tranquilizers, and he prepared injections of heart stimulants. Each pair worked for ten minutes then rested for ten. Finally, he brought in the smoke extractor to keep the air in the tunnel fresh.

Also during this period he set up and tested an elaborate lookout system.

Lookout number one was at street level close to the entrance to the underground parking lot, sitting in a Renault 5. In case of danger he was to run into the lot and through the siphon room to Marcel. Marcel would then run along the underground road and into the sewer, and blow a whistle.

Lookout number two was at the river entrance to the underground road, more than a mile away, sitting on a motorcycle. His instructions were to drive down the underground road, get off his bike, enter the sewer and blow a whistle.

So in case of danger from either entrance the men in the tunnel would have the opportunity to escape via the alternative entrance.

For double safety, the Renault 5 and the motorcycle were in radio contact. (Spaggiari would have liked radio contact with the vault, too, but the mass of concrete made this impossible.)

They tested the whistles and discovered that the men in the tunnel could hear them at a distance of two hundred yards through the sewers even with three blowtorches going at full blast.

They also timed the motorcyclist's journey from the entrance to the sewer. It took one minute and fifteen seconds.

ONE NIGHT in the first week of July the tunnelers struck the concrete wall of the bank vault. They cleared an area three feet across and put down their tools. The Mason completed his cementing and checked his work. Everything was ready.

The president's visit caused a postponement, but nobody discovered Spaggiari's tunnel. The incident at

Castagniers gave the team some bad moments, but the gendarmes seemed to drop the matter.

D-day was set for Friday 16 July.

The heist was on.

Getting In

4

QUAND LA REALITÉ
DÉPASSE LA FICTION . . .
(When Reality Surpasses Fiction . . .)
—headline in *Nice-Matin,* 21 July 1976

FRIDAY, 10:30 P.M.

THE CHINAMAN slammed on the brakes. The Land-Rover screeched to a halt. The four men in the back seat grabbed for the gas cylinders to stop them from falling over. The driver of the city bus, which had almost collided with the Land-Rover, shouted a muffled obscenity and drove on down the Rue de l' Hôtel des Postes. The Chinaman wiped his forehead with a checked handkerchief.

"Cunt," said one of the men.

"It wasn't my fault," said The Chinaman. "The stupid bus—"

"Just keep driving," said Albert Spaggiari, who was sitting in the front next to The Chinaman. "Nobody's blaming you. Take a left." With pretended nonchalance he put his feet on the dashboard and lit a cigar.

The Chinaman did not like the Land-Rover, but Spaggiari insisted on using it. It reminded him of the war in Indochina. The Chinaman did not like the war, either. In fact he did not like Spaggiari, who got on his nerves by playing the big shot.

He turned into the Avenue Pauliani and followed it to the Place du Quinzième Corps. At the Church Notre Dame Auxiliatrice he turned into the Avenue Dom Bosco. A high wall lined the street. Behind it was the city jail.

Spaggiari bit on the plastic tip of his cigar and turned to the men in the back. "We start from the prison. Is that a good omen?"

Nobody laughed. Henri the Welder held up crossed fingers. Then he started talking about the Tour de France bicycle race. The others joined in a little too eagerly. They were nervous.

Only a madman could have relaxed.

The jeep reached the bank of the Paillon and stopped. The red white and blue lamp of the *Gendarmerie*—a barracks, not a police station—was out. The town's exhibition hall in the distance was also in darkness. The Chinaman flashed his lights: two longs, one short. In the riverbed another light answered: two longs, one short. All clear.

The Chinaman steered down the access ramp and on to the sand of the riverbed. The man with the flashlight walked beside the Land-Rover. Another man moved the low barrier to the underground road, and the jeep bumped into the mouth of the tunnel and stopped.

Spaggiari jumped out. "Everything all right?"

"Yes." The man who answered pulled a walkie-talkie from inside his jacket, put it to his mouth, and pressed the transmit button. "This is Roseau," he said softly. "The move is complete. Over."

The radio crackled and replied: "This is Massena. Send us the furniture."

Spaggiari spoke to the man with the flashlight. "Where's the motorcycle?"

The man jerked his head backward. "Over there. Don't get excited."

Spaggiari raised his eyebrows. The man noticed the reaction in the light of his flashlight. "Sorry," he said quickly.

Spaggiari said: "If something happens—"

"I'll warn you in one minute and fifteen seconds."

"Then abandon the bike and disappear through the underground parking lot."

"Right."

Spaggiari climbed back into the Land-Rover. The

Chinaman flicked on the sidelights and rolled the jeep under the arch and into the tunnel. The motorcyclist and the man with the flashlight replaced the low barrier.

The Land-Rover gathered speed, and The Chinaman put the headlights on. The lights picked out the debris of a building site: cement bags, bricks, old newspapers, mortar boards. There had been talk of turning this road into a highway that would take traffic from the outskirts of the city right to the Promenade des Anglais, but the project never got off the drawing board. The only people who used the road were the workmen of the sewers department.

The jeep passed an arch on the left, through which could be heard the summer trickle of the Paillon River. A small army of rats blinked in the lights, then disappeared behind a stack of rotting wooden boards. The air smelled musty. Up ahead, the lights picked out a group of men standing, waiting. The Land-Rover slowed down and stopped beside them.

THE SECOND team had come in from the Place Massena, via the underground parking lot and the siphon room. They were carrying the rubber suits, the thigh-high waders, gloves, extra tools, plus two inflatable dinghies and several inner tubes for truck tires. Now they stood on the underground road, close to the entrance to the sewer system, and pumped up the inflatables.

In a nearby hotel room a doctor was settling down in an armchair. He was to be on call for the next sixty hours. He was not a real doctor, though he had been until the authorities discovered he was performing illegal abortions. Since he had lost his license he had found a little work with the *milieu*—attending to gunshot wounds when the victims had reason to avoid hospitals and policemen, that sort of thing. It didn't exactly keep him busy, but it paid the rent.

Spaggiari had not told the doctor precisely what was going on this weekend, but it was not difficult to guess. The medical problems he might have to deal with included asphyxiation, claustrophobia and mechanical injury. They must be digging a tunnel somewhere. The doctor did not want to know the details. On Monday morning he would take his money, go home and suffer an attack of selective amnesia. A man must make his living.

Nowadays abortion was being legalized in half the world, but that was the irony of life.

In the Avenue Verdun, close but not too close to the bank, was parked a Renault 4 exactly like the ones used by the electric company. Inside were five cylinders of gas and a hydraulic lever. The lever was an essential piece of equipment, but it was very heavy. Almost everything Spaggiari needed could be transported along the sewers themselves on the inflatable dinghies and the inner tubes; but the lever would have sunk the boats, so it had to go in via the manhole outside the bank. This would be the most risky part of the whole operation. The men in the Renault smoked nervously and waited for the word.

In the underground road the waiting men opened the back of the Land-Rover and pulled down the loading ramp. The atmosphere was tense: nobody spoke. Deliberately, Spaggiari shook hands with each of them, smiling, making small talk, jollying them out of their mood. It worked.

They unloaded the jeep and began to transfer the equipment to the convoy of inflatables. The Mason had brought along a couple of inflatable beach mattresses as well. The dinghies, the mattresses and the inner tubes were tied together like a string of barges. When the loading was complete the men stepped into the sewage and began the trek through the drains to the bank. The Mason went first.

They waded along, bent double—the drains were less than three feet in diameter—for one hundred yards beneath the Rue Chauvain; turned left beneath the Rue Gioffredo and right into the Rue St. Michel; and struggled on another two hundred yards to the bank. The Chinaman cursed: his boots kept getting stuck in the mud at the bottom of the sewer.

The convoy stopped at the entrance to the tunnel the gang had made. The Mason stepped into the tunnel and unrolled the rope carpet, which would make it easier to drag heavy equipment the length of the eight-yard tunnel to the wall of the vault. The others began to unload the inflatables.

The tunnel smelled of sewage and acetone. Henri the Welder leaned two gas cylinders against the wall, connected his blowtorch, and flipped down the blue shield of his goggles. He was giving The Corsican a last lesson.

He turned on the torch and flicked his cigarette lighter. The long orange flame cast giant shadows on the tunnel walls. "As you turn the flame down, it gets hotter." He demonstrated, and the torch began to burn blue and hiss.

He took a can of solder from his sea-bag and held the flame over it. "Always aim at the bottom, and torch in short bursts; otherwise the stuff will slip off the metal and won't stick."

There was a cry from the sewer: "Oh, *shit!*" It was The Chinaman.

Somebody laughed.

"What happened?"

"He slipped and got a bootful of sewage."

The laughter relieved the tension.

The equipment was stacked in the tunnel and the boats went back for another load. In the next ninety minutes, one ton of material was shifted from the underground road to the tunnel.

The Mason inspected his roof and found that some

of the supporting beams in the second half of the tunnel had sunk into the mud. He set about the job of making them firm. Back in the Place Massena parking lot someone plugged in the electric cable, and two floodlights suddenly came on in the tunnel.

A POLICE patrol car cruised across the Place Massena. In the Renault 5, the lookout lifted his walkie-talkie to his lips. "This is Massena. The seagull is flying low."

At the entrance to the underground road the other lookout replied: "Received." He called to the motorcyclist: "Cops near the underground parking lot."

The motorcyclist climbed on his machine and started it.

The patrol car passed the entrance of the lot and continued on to the Avenue Jean Médecin. The lookout in the Renault 5 laughed with relief. "All clear," he said into the walkie-talkie.

The motorcyclist turned his machine off.

SATURDAY, 1:30 A.M.

The Mason and The Corsican lay side-by-side in the tunnel, drilling. The two-hundred-watt floodlights and the power tools made the atmosphere terribly hot, and sweat poured off the muscular backs of the two men. The smoke extractor was working at full blast.

The reinforced concrete wall of the vault was a foot thick, but the team had penetrated half its thickness during the previous week. On the first night Spaggiari had stood outside the bank while the team in the tunnel operated four compression hammers simultaneously: he could hear nothing.

The Mason and The Corsican drilled fourteen holes at half-inch intervals. Then they crawled back to let The Chinaman in. Spaggiari handed them towels and bottles of mineral water, and they drank thirstily.

The Chinaman chipped away at the concrete with a hammer and chisel. He wore goggles, but a splinter had already gashed his check. He counted out fifty strokes with the large hammer, then thirty with the small one; then he crawled back and let P—— take his turn. Eighty strokes was all they could manage at one go.

Behind them a fifth man was shoveling the debris into bags and a sixth was carting it away in a wheelbarrow.

The Mason drained the bottle of water and put an arm around Spaggiari's shoulders. "What are we missing on TV tonight?"

" 'The Untouchables,' " Spaggiari said.

They all laughed.

P—— completed his eighty strokes and Spaggiari announced a break. He killed the floodlights, leaving only a small twenty-five-watt lamp burning, to let the air in the tunnel cool off. He took a vaccuum flask out of a bag and poured coffee for everyone.

The atmosphere was relaxed, but there had been a tense moment earlier. The men had been expecting to use the laser on the concrete wall, but Spaggiari had announced that it was not possible: the machine created too much heat, gas and smoke to be used safely in a confined space, especially without the required special clothing. He had only bought the machine to keep the men's spirits up. There had been mutinous grumbles when they discovered they faced another night of drilling and chiseling; but—as Spaggiari had calculated—they were too close to their goal to rebel now. The moment passed.

Marcel, the lookout from the siphon room, came in. "How's it going?"

"What are you doing here?" Spaggiari asked him.

"Roger took over for me." Roger was serving a three-year prison sentence in Marseilles, and had been allowed out on a weekend pass to visit his mother. Instead of going home he had decided to earn a million francs before returning to his cell.

"How's it going?" Marcel repeated.

P—— said: "The wall sounded a little hollow this time. I think we're almost there. We'll probably get through this time around."

SATURDAY, 10:30 A.M.

The chisels were blunt and the men were half dead, but the wall held out. Four men lay flat out on the rope carpet, too tired to move: The Mason, Henri the Welder, Marcel and Roger. In the sewer another eight men, wearing waders, were doing exercises to loosen cramped muscles: swinging their arms, stretching, swaying. The only thing they could not do was stand up straight.

Roger cursed. "We'll still be here tomorrow. We're going to have to use the laser."

"No," Spaggiari said firmly. "Don't you understand what a temperature of five thousand degrees would mean in a space like this? We'd all fry."

"We could set the machine up and wait in the sewer."

"The fumes would asphyxiate us. Also, the smoke would go up through the manholes into the street. We might as well give ourselves up to the police now."

There was a pregnant silence. Spaggiari lit a cigar. "Anyone who wants to quit only has to say so."

The Mason nodded wearily, got up, and returned to the wall. The Chinaman joined him.

Spaggiari concealed a sigh of relief. The crisis was past.

SATURDAY, 4:00 P.M.

"Holy Mother of God!"

The Mason was on the point of cracking up. The chisel seemed to be welded to the skin of his hand. His eyes were burning, he was too hot, and he desperately needed sleep. The concrete came away one piece at a time from the steel reinforcing ribs.

The Mason's control snapped. He slammed the chisel into the concrete and swung his hammer with all his might. The concrete crumbled; the chisel slipped through; and the force of the blow rammed both the handle of the chisel and The Mason's thumb into the space. The Mason screamed in agony and passed out.

They were through.

In a flash, Spaggiari was beside The Mason. Gently, he pulled the man's hand away from the hole. He shuddered: the thumb looked like a raw steak. He gave The Mason a shot of novocaine.

Only then did he look at the wall.

"What happened?" asked The Chinaman.

"We made it!" Spaggiari said. *"We're through the bastard wall!"*

Everyone began laughing and cheering.

IT TOOK another five hours to make the hole wide enough for a man to crawl through comfortably. The Mason was out of action, still taking drugs for the pain, but now nobody minded the work. When the last of the concrete was chipped off and carted away, The Chinaman attacked the steel ribs buried in the wall, cutting them with the oxyacetylene blowtorch and bending the stumps back out of the way.

When he was done, he beckoned Spaggiari.

Albert knelt on the rope carpet and peered into the hole. On the other side, as he had expected, was the back of one of the armored cabinets holding the safe-deposit boxes. Thirty tons, the guard had said it weighed. Spaggiari turned around and spoke to René. "Go ahead. Notify Marcel."

SATURDAY, 9:00 P.M.

René, who was called The Poet because of his romantic eyes and long hair, hurried along the sewer, his hands brushing the sides of the pipe. He reached the underground road and ran to the siphon room, where Marcel was waiting.

"The hydraulic lever," he panted.

Marcel went through the door into the underground parking lot, ran across to the stairs and went up into the street—the Rue Félix Faure. He lifted his flashlight, pointed it across the street, and gave two short flashes.

The waiting Renault 5 replied with two short flashes of its headlights, then moved off and swung into the

Avenue Verdun. The Renault 4, which looked like an electric company van, was waiting there, lights off. The Renault 5 tooted sharply as it passed the smaller car.

Captain V——, the Vietnam veteran, and G——, the Algerian, were not in the van, but were sitting nearby on the low wall around the Albert I park. They had waited almost twenty-four hours—much longer than expected. They watched the Renault 5 disappear into the Rue Paradis then got into the van.

In the front seat, they struggled into the blue overalls and matching caps of electricity workmen. The Algerian started the van.

They stopped at a red light on the Promenade des Anglais outside the Meridian Hotel. At the curb two policemen were talking to three motorcyclists, examining their licenses. The light turned green.

The Algerian drove on around the block. Avenue des Phocéens, Place Massena, Rue Gioffredo, Rue St. Michel . . . the van stopped at the corner of the Rue Gustave Deloye and the Rue de l'Hôtel des Postes. The Algerian killed the engine and both men got out.

They moved fast but tried to act naturally, as if they had every right to be there. Across the street the evening drinkers at the Taverne Alsacienne watched idly from their pavement tables.

The Algerian placed a blue light and a "Danger—Men at Work" sign beside the manhole. Captain V—— took a pick out of the back of the van and used it to lift the manhole cover. The lid was marked with the Pontamousson brand name. He slid into the hole.

The Algerian lifted the hydraulic lever from the back of the van with considerable effort. It weighed one hundred pounds. Carefully, he lowered it into the manhole.

Captain V——took the weight, then passed the lever on to the men waiting in the sewer below him.

He got out of the manhole and replaced the lid.

The two men in blue overalls picked up the light and the danger sign and got back into the van. The Algerian started the engine and pulled away.

The van had been parked for precisely twenty-six seconds.

IN THE sewer, someone turned the light back on. The Chinaman and The Corsican had the lever on their shoulders. Cautiously, awkwardly, they carried it along the drain to the mouth of the tunnel. The Mason directed them: his ruined thumb was bandaged and his arm was in a sling.

They lowered the lever on to the rope carpet and dragged it the length of the tunnel to the hole in the vault wall.

Roger, the prisoner on a forty-eight-hour pass, was fixing a brace for the lever. He had selected a heavy timber and jammed it upright between the floor and the roof of the tunnel.

Spaggiari and P——lifted the lever, wedging its

base against the wooden brace and maneuvering its head through the hole in the wall. The Chinaman began to pump the lever. Its head touched the back of the thirty-ton steel cabinet inside the vault, and the lever took the strain. Gingerly, Spaggiari and P—— let go. The lever was wedged.

The Chinaman carried on pumping. The cabinet had to move almost two feet. Spaggiari had calculated this distance precisely: twenty inches. It would be enough to let the men through, but not enough to make the cabinet tip over and fall on its face.

The Chinaman began to perspire freely. P—— measured the distance the safe had moved so far. René was holding a timber prop exactly twenty inches long.

"Okay—that's it," said P——. The cabinet had moved approximately twenty-one inches. René eased his prop into the space alongside the lever, and The Chinaman loosened the lever.

With painful slowness the steel cabinet tilted backward and came to rest on Reneé's prop. The prop creaked, pushing hard against the brace in the tunnel, but it held.

The Chinaman lowered the hydraulic lever to the floor.

Spaggiari crawled through the hole and into the bank vault.

Getting Out

5

A PORN AND PÂTÉ PARTY FOR
GANGSTER MILLIONAIRES
—headline in the London *Daily Express*

SUNDAY, 2:00 A.M.

SPAGGIARI'S TORCH threw a faint beam over the furniture of the vault: steel tables, old chairs, armored cabinets. It was a dead world.

Henri the Welder was second through the hole, dragging his blowtorch and gas tanks behind him. He knew what to do. Swiftly, without speaking, he crossed to the vault door. He lit his torch, then carefully welded the door to its frame. Now, in the unlikely event that bank officials should have reason to enter the vault during Sunday, they would find the door stuck and give the gang plenty of time to get away.

The Corsican covered the doorframe with plastic cement, sealing the cracks. He did the same with the ventilation grilles in the vault walls. Now no light, smoke or noise could penetrate to the outside world.

Only then did Spaggiari switch on the lights.

The rest of the team entered the vault rapidly, bringing the equipment with them, and went to work with a will.

The Boxer used a steel hacksaw to cut down the iron portcullis that separated the safe-deposit room from the treasury room; then did the same for the similar partition closing off the night safe.

The Chinaman and The Corsican went to work on the safes. They melted the hinges, then burned a six-inch hole in the door for leverage. Finally they wrenched the door open with picks and mallets. Once inside the cabinet, it was a simple matter to open the individual safe-deposit boxes by softening up the thin doors with the torch, buckling them with a hammer, and prying them open with a crowbar.

The hysteria hit them all at once.

One moment the team was working efficiently, quietly, professionally; tensely aware of the danger they were in, concentrating on getting as much treasure as they could in the twenty-four hours or so they had left. Next moment they were all laughing fit to burst.

All of them, down to the most amateurish *demi sel,* had been building up to this moment for weeks. The strain of more than a day in the tunnel, trying to break through the vault wall, had screwed their nerves up tight as a drum. Now, suddenly, it hit them that they had made it: they were inside Ali Baba's cave, protected from the world by a welded steel door, casually helping themselves to undreamed-of riches—stacks of gold bars, bags full of bank notes, heaps of priceless jewels.

They went bananas.

They roared with laughter, slapped each other on the back and embraced. The Poet was seized with a trembling fit. The Chinaman grabbed a fistful of Pinay—government securities—and threw them in the air, yelling: "Confetti!" The others followed his lead. Stock certificates, IOUs, contracts, wills, bank notes and negotiable securities flew through the air. It was like a slapstick movie.

Only Spaggiari and The Mason stood aside from it all. The Mason, who was still in pain from his crushed thumb, grumbled: "Those bits of paper are worth money. Some of them are bearer bonds—anyone can cash them. There's practically no risk."

"Hey, forget them, will you?" Spaggiari said. "We'll have more than we can carry in cash, gold and gems."

"I don't see the point of throwing money away."

Spaggiari said firmly: "We decided all that beforehand. We're only taking gold, cash, precious stones and jewelry. Now just *forget* it."

He decided the hysteria had gone on long enough

now. He moved around the vault, speaking to individuals in a low voice, calming them down. When the place was quiet again he said: "All right, let's take a good long break and have dinner."

The idea was greeted with general acclamation. They had gone for almost thirty-six hours with no more than an occasional square of chocolate and a few gulps of mineral water. Now Spaggiari, like a magician producing rabbits out of a hat, brought out pâté, salami, garlic sausage, TV dinners, dehydrated soups, cheese, dates, grapes and oranges.

The Mason put a saucepan of mineral water to boil on the portable stove and said: "Who wants bacon-and-pea soup?"

Someone said: "Next time you'll have to bring an oven and bake us a cake."

The Chinaman found a cellophane-wrapped pizza. "Junk food," he said scornfully. Then he discovered the goose liver pâté and seized it with glee.

Henri the Welder set up a picnic on the steel table. Papers from the safe-deposit boxes formed his tablecloth. His menu: fish, raw onions, pâté, yogurt and zwieback biscuits.

Spaggiari picked up a gold dish with the coat-of-arms of a noble family and handed it to The Mason. "I'll take a little of that soup, please."

The Poet opened the wine, a Margnat Village, and poured some into a silver goblet for Henri the Welder.

"We could afford better than this," Henri said.

"Perhaps Monsieur would have preferred the Mouton Rothschild '47, or maybe the Gevrey Chambertin '59?" The Poet replied. "Does Monsieur not think we had enough junk to drag through that bloody sewer?"

The Corsican was sitting on a gas cylinder looking through some photographs he had found in a safe-deposit box and sipping a glass of wine. "I've seen better," he said, and showed them around. They were amateur pornography, showing naked, mainly middle-aged people involved in various sexual contortions. Some of the faces were recognizable. They all looked faintly ridiculous.

"These are top people," someone said in astonishment. "We should expose them." He stuck a few of the pictures on the wall.

Spaggiari called to The Mason, who was making himself useful as cook since he could no longer help with the heavy work. "Hey, waiter, how about some coffee?"

"Coming right up, sir."

Spaggiari handed out cigars and cigarettes.

Suddenly someone said: "Hush! For God's sake, *listen!*"

The room went dead still.

They all heard, quite clearly, a faint but distinct noise coming from the night safe.

Spaggiari tiptoed across the vault and entered the small triangular room from which the noise had come.

THE WHITE Rolls-Royce pulled up in the Rue de l'Hôtel des Postes and three men got out. One was the bagman, and the other two were his bodyguards. All three were young, large, athletic and armed. They looked nervously about the moonlit street, as anyone will look around nervously when he is in charge of one hundred seventy-five thousand dollars, no matter how young, large, athletic and armed he may be.

The takings of a long Saturday night at the casino were in the bag. The usual Nice gambling crowd had been there, plus the tourists: English, German, American and Arab. Especially Arab.

The three men in the Rolls did not know exactly how much was in the bag, for someone else had counted it and filled up the forms and sealed the containers; but they knew it was a lot, a sum of money well worth killing for.

They crossed the pavement to the wall of the bank. The two bodyguards looked up and down the street while the bagman opened the steel flap in the wall, keyed the shutter behind it, and dropped the bag into the safe.

The three men relaxed. The money was safe.

They got into the car and drove away.

THE BAG fell down the chute and into Spaggiari's waiting arms.

He touched his forehead in a subservient gesture and said: "Thank you very much, sir. Sleep well."

The others thought it was hilarious.

Spaggiari broke open the bag and looked through the money. "About a million francs," he said casually. "Must be casino takings."

He put out his cigar and went back to work on the safe-deposit boxes. The others followed suit. They were running out of time.

Once again Spaggiari imposed a shift system, forcing his men to take regular breaks for rest and refreshment. The Chinaman wanted to work on, but Albert would not hear of it. "We're treading on each other's toes, anyway."

The air in the vault became foul, despite the smoke extractor, and Spaggiari had to work hard to keep morale high.

At one point Roger came in from the tunnel. "The water is rising out there. Must be a storm."

"We're safe," The Mason told him. "There are storm drains. Besides, the lookouts will warn us if it gets too high."

Roger decided to have a snack. "Goose liver pâté, nothing but goose liver pâté," he joked. "What kind of food is that to give a prisoner?"

SUNDAY, 10:00 P.M.

The jeweler came in via the underground parking lot. Marcel led him through the sewers to the vault. Distastefully he shook the dirty water off his waders. He was a fastidious man with effeminate gestures.

Marcel showed him the jewels. His expression of distaste changed to one of greed, almost lust, as he began to examine the stones. He put his glass to his eye. Diamonds, rubies, sapphires, emeralds, gold and silver: he had never seen so much wealth in his life. Some of the stuff he tossed aside as being hardly worth the trouble of fencing. The best stones he put into black velvet bags, and the little velvet bags disappeared into a larger blue bag. Every now and then he took a sip of mineral water. He was valuing the loot as he went. "Five hundred thousand francs . . . and fifty is five hundred-fifty thousand . . . and eight thousand is six hundred and thirty thousand francs . . . and twenty . . ."

They discovered a faster way to get at the safe-deposit boxes. Some of the cabinets were doubles, with a door at the front and another door at the back. Instead of opening both the front door and the back door, they realized they could take all the boxes out of the front half of the safe then go through the thin partition to the backs of the other set of boxes, thereby saving the heavy work of breaking open another safe door.

Spaggiari assigned four men—The Poet, Captain V——, Roger the Prisoner and The Boxer—to sorting out the rest of the loot. They wrapped the gold ingots carefully, using the paper their tools had been wrapped in. Cash and jewelry went into the black plastic bags Spaggiari had brought.

Roger said: "Do we have to leave all the tools here?"

"What else would we do with them?" The Chinaman replied. "Sell them in the flea market?"

MONDAY, 5:00 A.M.

"That's it," Spaggiari called. "Time to go."

The Mason turned off the gas to the torches. Henri the Welder pushed his goggles up to his forehead. His face was covered with soot, sweat and dust, and his eyes were red-rimmed.

"Already?" Henri said. He checked his watch. "Christ, it's morning."

They had got into fewer than four hundred of the four thousand safe-deposit boxes. In a way it was frustrating to have to leave so much wealth untouched. But when he thought about what they already had, it hardly seemed to matter what was left behind.

Spaggiari was organizing the departure. The loot was carried through the tunnel and loaded on to the inflatables. The Poet suggested removing the beam that had held up the tilted safe all weekend. "Then it will take them even longer to discover how we got in." Spaggiari was not interested: he just wanted to get out fast, now.

The Mason was the last to leave the vault. He turned out the light.

THE CONVOY of dinghies, mattresses and inner tubes, now loaded with gold, cash and jewelry, was towed back through the sewers to the underground road. There the loot was transferred to the Land-Rover. On the way the men discarded gloves, goggles and assorted tools.

They were taking off their waterproof overalls and disappearing in ones and twos through the underground parking lot.

Henri the Welder, The Corsican, and Spaggiari got into the Land-Rover. The Chinaman started the engine and looked back. The Mason, who was still changing his clothes, signaled with his bandaged thumb. The jeep pulled away.

The Chinaman killed the headlights when he saw the light of day at the far end of the underground road. The motorcyclist, still on lookout duty, gave the all-clear signal. Henri and The Corsican jumped out of the car and moved the barrier.

The Chinaman drove out into the new day.

The motorcyclist climbed on to his machine and drove away. Henri and The Corsican replaced the barrier to the underground road and got back into the Land-Rover.

The Chinaman drove across the sandy riverbed and up the ramp into the street. The Land-Rover passed the exhibition hall and disappeared in the direction of Laudimères.

The city was just waking up. Outside the bank, a street sweeper was clearing the pavement along the Rue Gustave Deloye. The cafés were pulling up their blinds. The sun was edging into the sky over the Baie des Anges.

It was going to be a hot day.

The Investigation Begins

6

Partez en vacances, sans souci, louez un coffre à la Société Générale.
(Go on holiday without fear—rent a safe-deposit box at the Société Générale).
—advertisement

THIS IS the banker's nightmare: he stands alone, inside a deserted bank, behind locked and barred doors; while outside, on the pavement, a huge crowd of angry depositors shout curses and demand their money back.

The nightmare of the robbery had leaked out the previous afternoon when a detective talked to a reporter from *Nice-Matin.* At 5:30 P.M. Guy Salignon, newscaster on the Europe number one radio station, had broadcast a special bulletin. By 5:45 the news was on Radio Monte Carlo, and then within minutes half the world's newspapers were on the phone to Nice.

The crowd began to gather outside the bank around 9:00 P.M. Some of them stayed all night. By 8:30 A.M. they were ready to riot.

One woman fainted. Another sat on the curb, quietly weeping. There was talk of lynching Guenet. A well-dressed young man was hanging onto the wrought iron gate like a madman, shouting. He calmed down to explain to reporters: "My father has a safe-deposit box in there with his life savings in it. He is eighty years old. If I can't reassure him—if I can't tell him his money is safe—it will kill him."

A hysterical customer screamed at the crowd-control police: "You're treating us as if we were the thieves."

As bank employees arrived the crowd spat at them. The police made halfhearted attempts to move people on, but they simply staged a sit-down strike on the pavement. The well-dressed young man moved his car into a no-parking zone and refused to budge.

One customer brought with him a *luissier de justice*—an official combining the functions of an English bailiff with those of an American notary public. He demanded to see his box, and almost came to blows with a bank employee. Finally he turned to the *luissier* and said: "Please witness that they prevented me seeing my box and refused all cooperation."

In vain bank officials explained that the vault had to be cleared up, and the police had given strict instructions that no one was to be admitted. "Tell that to the cleaning woman," someone shouted.

At last Guenet issued a communiqué. Only a small proportion of the safe-deposit boxes had been opened, he said. However, he would not give out a list of the numbers. Instead he named the approximate numerical areas within which boxes had been robbed. He asked customers with boxes in those areas to submit an inventory of the contents of their box, and assured them that all claims would be met.

The inventories would be dealt with by the police.

This plan infuriated the customers even more, but from the bank's point of view it was the only possible course of action. This way nobody could be *certain* that his box had been robbed, and therefore nobody would be tempted to submit a dishonest inventory claiming compensation far above what he had lost. Nevertheless, the customers considered the bank was treating them like thieves.

Many of them simply resented being asked for an inventory. "I rent a safe-deposit box for security *and* privacy," said one. "They promised me this when I rented it. Not only have they failed to give me security: they also demand that my personal business is exposed to every nosey cop in Nice."

Some customers were now satisfied. "I know what was in my safe and I can prove it. I've nothing to hide. The bank is insured, and I will be reimbursed. Everyone will. There's nothing to worry about."

Another customer: "The vault is like the Maginot

Line: it has been invaded from the other side. I take off my hat to the thieves: if only roadworks could be done so neatly."

One customer succeeded in getting through to Guenet, who told him: "I won't tell you anything. I've done my duty." The customer repeated this tactless remark to reporters.

The bank's public relations clumsiness was not helped by the five thousand advertising brochures that had been distributed not long before the raid. Beneath a photograph of a plundered apartment the caption ran: "Go on holiday without fear—rent a safe-deposit box at the Société Générale."

There was to be more delay. The police would accept claims at 1 Avenue Foch from July 28 onward. Customers were instructed to attend with their identity papers and their inventories.

Seven of the three hundred-and-seventeen victims declined to make a claim. One man made a false claim and was paid two hundred thousand francs for lost jewelry; but he returned the money after he discovered his wife had removed the jewelry from the box when she ran off with another man.

Adding insult to injury, the bank compared the value of each inventory with the state of the customer's bank account, and queried cases where the customer seemed too poor to have so much wealth in a safe-deposit box.

At last the bank began to pay out: five customers per

day. Before receiving his indemnity each one had to sign a promise that he would return the money in the event that his possessions were recovered and returned to him.

The directors of the bank issued another communiqué, apologizing for the robbery. The customers received it with a mixture of contempt and hysterical laughter.

The Société Générale lost a lot of customers.

The losers were also called in to identify the valuables that the thieves had left strewn around the strongroom floor.

On July 23 the bank's Paris headquarters stepped in to rescue its reputation before it was too late. The director general, Monsieur Laure, announced a reward of one million francs for information leading to the conviction of the robbers. He hoped it would give a shot in the arm to the police investigation.

The investigation badly needed it.

THERE WERE very few clues—or perhaps it would be more accurate to say there were hundreds of clues, but none of them led anywhere.

Most of the equipment left behind consisted of commonplace tools that might have been bought in any of a thousand shops in France. The screwdrivers were marked "Kilt"—the brand name of the Nouvelles Galeries chain of stores, which sold thousands of such screwdrivers every year. The gas cylinders for the oxyacetylene torches were numberd, and so could be traced back to the manufacturer; but they turned out to have been stolen from a building site at Vitrolles, near Marseilles. Some of the pickaxes had tungsten heads, which made them slightly unusual. Detectives went around the hardware stores. "An excellent choice," the proprietors would say. "The best on the market. We sell dozens of them. I couldn't possibly remember all the customers." The canvas sea-bags were identified as coming from a department store in Milan which had sold hundreds of them. And so on.

The fingerprint men dusted the whole of the vault and every item of equipment found. Of course, there were hundreds of prints all over the safes and the boxes where customers had handled them. But on the tools, the torches, the gas cylinders, the inflatables and even the wine bottles there was not a single fingerprint. *All* the thieves had worn gloves *all* the time.

The mineral water bottles in which the thieves had urinated were sent away for chemical analysis. But the gang had thought even of that, and the laboratory reported that nothing could be discovered from the urine because *more than one person had urinated in every single bottle.*

Hopes were briefly raised when a member of the public walked into the police station at 1 Avenue Foch and announced that he had seen the gang.

"I was having a drink at a sidewalk table at the Taverne Alsacienne on Saturday night. A Renault 4 parked outside the bank, and two men lifted the manhole cover. I didn't pay any attention—I just assumed they were doing some urgent electrical repairs.'

"Can you describe the men?"

"They were wearing blue overalls. That's all I saw."

At first the detectives thought they might find a shopkeeper who remembered selling over three hundred yards of electrical cable to one customer; then they discovered that the cable consisted of several forty-yard and fifty-yard lengths joined together.

The police were reduced to soliciting information from the pimps, prostitutes, dope dealers and *demi sels* in the cafés and bars of the Old Town. Now they were handicapped by too much information: *everyone* boasted that he had had a hand in the heist of the century, and all those boasts reached the ears of the detectives. None of the information was reliable, and there were far too many names to be checked out. It was another kind of dead end.

The public rejoiced in the success of the robbery, and the mystery brain behind it became a kind of national hero. (Something similar happened in the British case of the Great Train Robbery; although here the gangsters' image was tarnished by the subsequent death of a railwayman who had been roughly handled during the heist. However, the Sewer Rats injured nobody.)

The police leaked a story that the brain might be

Italian. They were shooting in the dark, and everyone knew it.

In fact they used their computer in an effort to identify the brain. Given the basic details of the job, the computer produced a list of known top criminals who might, on past form, have been able to organize the heist. The police checked on each of them. Some were in jail, others were out of the country, all had excellent, credible alibis.

Seven days after the heist the Société Générale received an anonymous phone call. The caller would give the police a complete list of the participants in the coup if the bank would double its reward.

The bank dithered. One million francs on delivery of the list, one million on recovery of the stolen money, it suggested.

The negotiations went on for a while but finally broke down. In the meantime the caller had supplied a list of initials, as a token of good faith.

At the top of the list were the initials "A.S."

ON THE morning of July 20 Patrick Gruau bought his copy of *Nice-Matin,* as usual, at the shop across the street from the *Gendarmerie.* The front-page headline read: EXTRAORDINARY ROBBERY OF NICE BANK.

He rushed into the office and held the paper up. "They robbed the Société Générale at Nice!"

Chief Pierre Dufour looked up from his typewriter. "Robbed? How? A holdup?"

"No, no: a burglary. Here, read this." Gruau spread the newspaper on the table in front of his boss. The other gendarmes read over Dufour's shoulders. They all had the same thought in mind: was this the "big job" in which the four strangers in Castagniers were said to be involved?

Dufour read the newspaper story several times, digesting every detail. Finally he said: "No, it's not possible."

"Not possible," Gruau echoed.

Claude Destreil said: "They looked very worried, though."

Dufour pushed his typewriter away, stood up, stretched his small tanned body, and picked up his cap. "I'm going to the villa," he said. "Destreil, double-check those names with criminal records. Gruau, come with me in the van. Sloma and Sanchez, if we're not back by midday, take care of the traffic at the Vesubie crossroads. Let's go."

The blue car followed Route Nationale 202 along the bank of the Var River. Gruau drove. Both men contemplated the delightful prospect of catching the bank robbers who had baffled the *Police Judiciare.* Gendarmes always feel hard done by. They collect information meticulously, leaving nothing to chance; sort, analyze and file it; then present it to the detectives who collect all the credit. It is the detectives who get medals, give television interviews and meet celebrities. The gendarmes are dogsbodies, at the beck and call of the city police, getting less money—they feel—for more work. Their strength lies in their intimate knowledge of their area, and the fact that they are prepared to check on such trivia as an unoccupied villa whose shutters are inexplicably open.

Dufour's suspicions had grown since the incident at the villa. He knew the owner, and the more he thought about it the less likely it seemed that that man would let someone use it for a stag party. Another thing: the man without papers had said his name was Alain Pons, but the records office had said there was no one in France with that name.

The gendarmes had kept an eye on the villa over the last few days, but had seen nothing unusual.

The little blue car entered the drive. There were tracks of a large vehicle in front of the garage, but they were not recent. The two men looked around, peeping through windows.

"Hello!"

They turned to see an elderly man with a hoe in his hand approaching them. His cap was pulled low to protect his eyes from the sun. He was Félix Maurel, and he lived next door. He was a good neighbor, if a trifle inquisitive, and he hoped nothing was wrong . . .

"Nothing special," Dufour told him in the close-mouthed manner of policemen everywhere. "But tell me, do you know anything about the people who were here eight days ago?"

"Not really," the old man said with a shrug. "I assume they were friends of the owner's. There were five or six of them, I think, but I'm not sure of that. For a while they were coming and going at all hours of the day and night, but it's been a while since I saw any of them."

Monsieur Maurel went back to his tomatoes and the gendarmes moved on.

They went to the café where their friend the illegal bookmaker hung out. He was hunched over the bar, checking the racing tips in the newspaper. When the gendarmes came in he moved out to the entrance.

Dufour and Gruau nodded to some of the clientele. A delivery boy carrying a crate of beer called out: "Hey, chief, are you following-up a clue?"

"Professional secret," Dufour replied with a smile.

They made small talk with the proprietor, listening to his grumbles about low profits and inventing a story about a stolen car to cover their presence in the café.

On their way out they passed the informer on the terrace. He was sitting under a sun-bleached parasol, as if his only interest in the world was the day's racing. The two gendarmes paused by his table to put on their caps.

"That coup I mentioned," he said without looking at them. "It's the one in Nice."

The gendarmes returned to their car.

AT MIDDAY on Tuesday the Nice detectives were awaiting the arrival from Paris of Contrôleur

Général Honoré Gevaudan, who was to supervise their inquiry.

In Scotland, Commissaire Divisionnaire Albert Mouray, forty-five, chief of the Nice police, had cut short his fishing holiday and was packing his bags to catch the next flight to Nice.

In London a *Daily Express* reporter was on the phone to *Nice-Matin,* trying to establish whether the heist was bigger than the Great Train Robbery.

It was.

In Marseilles General Mathieu, head of the serious crime squad, was packing for Nice.

In the same town the head of the Marseilles Mob was wondering whether he had misjudged Albert Spaggiari.

Spaggiari himself, and his team, were drinking champagne and counting gold bars, confident in their triumph.

And Dufour and Gruau, the village police who would ultimately cause Spaggiari's downfall, were sitting in a small blue van, sweltering in a traffic jam.

The Clues Come In

7

He was such a sweet child.
—Spaggiari's mother

IT WAS going to be a lengthy investigation.

Albert Mouray did not mind that. The chief of the Nice police was not unhappy with the prospect of weeks of inquiries, masses of information, the painstaking pursuit of small clues. He was a competent administrator rather than a brilliant detective. He had a tendency to go by the book, and those who wished to be cruel said it was typical of him to be on holiday when the heist of the century took place in his town.

His deputy, Claude Besson, *was* a brilliant detective. The financial expert was also content to settle down to a long investigation. He had made his reputation with such inquiries, and he was no stranger to the processes of compiling, sifting and comparing information.

They had plenty of help.

Doing the spadework, the nitty-gritty of detection, were two younger men, both highly skilled policemen, but very different characters.

Commissaire Eduard Taligault was brainy but vain. He spent a lot of time at the posh Ruhl Plage beach, nourishing his suntan. He was very upper-middle-class, with a somewhat superior manner. He was both a sportsman and an intellectual.

Commissaire Jacques Tholance was a complete contrast. When the American cop show "Colombo" appeared on French television, Tholance's colleagues laughed and said: *"Voilà, Jacques!"* He was short, thin and scruffy, and wore a shabby raincoat. He spent his evenings in the *louche* bars of the Old Town, picking up snippets of information. He was a great charmer—especially with women—and was very popular with the press, with whom he was cooperative. He was also greatly respected by the underworld.

Their first target was Monsieur V——; the trucking company owner with a jealous wife. The gendarmes had turned their information—such as it was—over to the detectives, and it was the best lead they had. Monsieur V—— seemed to be the centerpiece in the mystery of the villa at Castagniers.

The villa was a very plausible headquarters for a

gang. It was out in the country, yet handy for the town of Nice, for the airport, and for the main road to Lyons. It could be reached via several different major and minor roads, so that frequent comings and goings might be relatively unnoticed.

The whispers from Jacques Tholance's underworld contacts also favored Monsieur V——. He did not merely offer the use of a house, they said: he was deeply involved in the heist. He did not need the money, but he did it for kicks. He was an adventurer. He had been in the tunnel, digging . . . he had injured his hand . . .

However, there were scores of similar whispers about other people. The heist had been done by left-wing militants, the terrorist Carlos, the Red Brigades, right-wing militants . . .

In addition, members of the public came in in droves to report suspicious behavior by other members of the public. By and large the informers were elderly people and the suspicious behavers were young and long-haired. Nice's retired residents blame most things on the hippies, the blue-jeaned youngsters who sleep rough; but the hippies' only serious crime is to sell marijuana to the town's middle-class trendies.

So, at 10:00 A.M. on July 27, eight days after the heist, Judge Richard Bouazis stamped a search warrant for the villa in Castagniers.

Eduard Taligault was there at the office in the Promenade Corniglion Molinier to pick up the warrant. He went straight to the villa in his black Peugeot 204. Waiting for him there were the gendarmes from the Plan du Var station, the forensic team and the fingerprint boys from Nice, and Monsieur V——, who still had the key.

The house was filthy. The upholstery was stained and the Italian stone floor covered with black shoemarks. The ashtrays overflowed with cigarette and cigar butts and ash. The atmosphere was rank.

Taligault noted that none of the butts bore lipstick marks, then ordered the forensic team to have the tobacco analyzed.

In the kitchen he found a half-empty bottle of Margnat Village wine. A whole case of the same wine turned up in the garage.

Also in the garage was a heavy industrial heater of the kind used to dry up damp or flooded rooms. The heater's rubber base was covered with dried mud.

Monsieur V—— went around checking the locks on the windows and doors. A detective joked: "Afraid you've been robbed?" Nobody smiled.

On the way back, someone said: "Well, if there were any women there, we know for certain that either they didn't smoke or they didn't use lipstick. That's a clue."

He was being overly pessimistic.

The wine was the same brand as that found in the robbed vault.

The cigar butts were Havana tobacco, probably Don Miguel brand; again the same as those found in the vault.

And—the clincher—the mud on the base of the industrial heater had come from the sewers of Nice.

Taligault had found the gang's headquarters.

THE INTERROGATION of Monsieur V—— was brief and fruitless.

"Who borrowed the key from you?"

"Dominique Poggi."

"Why did he rent it?"

"He was going to have a party."

"Did you believe that?"

"Why shouldn't I?"

"Why didn't you tell the owner what you were doing?"

"No special reason. I keep an eye on the villa, and in return he lets me use it. I don't have to ask his permission every time."

"But *you* weren't using it—you gave the key to someone else."

Shrug.

"What have you done to your hand?"

"A riding accident."

"Who bandaged it?"

"I went to a clinic in Marseilles."

"Why so far away? What was so secret?"

"I went riding in the Camargue. I had the hand

attended to on the way back."

"Weren't you suspicious about a group of men holding a party without women?"

Shrug.

"Do you normally lend houses to people you hardly know?"

"They looked honest."

"Would you describe yourself as naïve?"

"I suppose so."

THE WAY to handle this case, decided Chief of Police Albert Mouray, was to spread a wide net. He would identify a large number of suspects, including those against whom there might be next to no evidence; then pick them up all at the same time and sort them out afterward.

His starting point was the information from the gendarmes. There were twelve names: Dominique Poggi, Daniel Michelucci, Christian Duche, "Alain Pons" (a false name), Monsieur and Madame V—— and their son, Raymond the café owner, the musical instrument salesman who owned the metallic-gray Peugeot, and the owners of the Mercedes, the Renault 17 and the Renault 5 that had reversed over the neighbor's lawn.

All of them were located, and were followed day and night. Notes were made of the people they met, and some of those—especially close associates or people with criminal records—were also followed. The list of names grew longer . . .

LEA WORE high-heeled boots, extremely tight hot-pants, and a camisole that hardly covered her large breasts. She was heavily made-up, and her breath smelled of whiskey. She walked slowly up and down a short stretch of the Promenade des Anglais, swinging a handbag.

Lea was a hustler.

It was eleven o'clock on a warm summer night and the promenade was crowded, but Lea's mind was not on her work tonight. She had good news, and she was bursting to share it.

She decided to take a break, and went into a bar in the Rue Maccarani for another whiskey. The bar's clientele was mixed: students, musicians, lawyers, whores and petty criminals. Odile was there: the perfect listener. Lea bought her a drink.

"You're not going to believe this: my man's taking an apartment in the Marine des Anges! It's classy, expensive and incredibly ugly!"

Odile was not sure whether to believe her. It was a very expensive area. Arabs and other wealthy foreigners lived there. It was difficult to imagine Lea and her man moving in among the Cadillacs, mink coats and Picasso lithographs.

"It's true!" Lea insisted. "It has air conditioning and fancy furniture and beautiful rugs . . ." She told Odile the name of the agency with which her man was dealing, the address of the apartment, the price tag, everything. Then she said: "I can trust you not to tell anyone, can't I? My man pulled something big. He says I can stop hustling. But you mustn't tell a soul."

Before the night was out half the whores on the promenade knew about Lea's good luck.

Two days later Lea's man, Francis Pellegrin, was under surveillance.

MIREILLE, THE secretary, slipped the contract form into her Olivetti and typed in the customer's name: Pellegrin, Francis. He had taken a beautiful apartment at Juan les Pins: marble floors, a lot of glass and wood, a view of the beach. Rent: eight hundred dollars per month, plus extras.

He did not look like a rich man, but he had hardly looked at the apartment, and he signed the contract without asking about the extras. He paid three months rent in advance, all in fifty-franc and hundred-franc notes, and left in a hurry.

Mireille was not completely surprised when, soon afterward, the police came in and asked to look at the contract.

PELLEGRIN HAD hurried away because he had a dental appointment in Cannes. He had his teeth capped, Hollywood-style. Soon afterward the police asked the dentist how much it had cost. Almost twenty-two hundred dollars he told them.

At a little after midnight on the first floor of a small hotel in the Rue de Pournet at Toulon, Michele Seaglie was making her bed. She plumped up the pillow and tidied the patchwork quilt. Dressed in soft suede boots and panties, she sat down in front of the mirror to make up her face.

She was beautiful, elegant and discreet. Her phone number was passed from one man to another in between the cheese and the fruit at business lunches. She knew how to behave in high society, she knew when to talk and when to keep her mouth shut, and one could appear with her in public without embarrassment. She had an apartment in Marseilles and a villa in Bandol. She had a lot of class.

Michelle was a hustler.

She put on a white see-through blouse and a colorful gypsy skirt, and tied her hair back. Then she left the room, locking it behind her, and went down the stairs to the street, where she had begun her career.

She smiled at Isis and Marlene, two beginners in her profession. Isis, the Asian girl, said: "Coming with us tonight?"

"Not me," Michele smiled, and she walked on.

She did not notice an old Renault 12 pull away from the curb and follow her. Inside were chief inspectors Thomasset and Spyron. Spyron, known as The Greek, lit a Gauloise and said: "That Daniel Michelucci's got damn good taste in women." He had said it before.

They had been following Michele for seven days and nights.

They watched her climb into a Renault 5 and put her seat belt on. They followed the car along the Boulevard de Strasbourg. At one point they were close enough to hear the music from her tape deck: it was Fats Domino singing "Blueberry Hill." But when she got out onto the freeway she put her foot down, and the detectives' ancient Renault would not catch her.

Frustrated, Thomasset drove back to the center of Toulon. "Today we should get the new Simca 1501. Then we'll see if she can lose us so easily."

ALBERT SPAGGIARI had arranged, long before the heist, to market the gold ingots from the strong room. They were to be sold at thirty percent below the market price—a very reasonable deal for stolen gold. However, Alain Bournat did not think it was a reasonable deal. This is because Alain Bournat was extremely stupid.

He insisted on keeping his share of the gold. Gold was the safest thing to invest in, he had heard. Foolishly, Spaggiari let him have his way.

At first Bournat tried to sell the gold to a man called Tschoa. Tschoa had a bar in the harbor at Nice. During the day it served sandwiches and coffee to the office workers in the area, but at night the curtains were drawn, champagne and Chivas Regal were served, and a few well-known clients played poker and barbutté for unusually high stakes.

Tschoa did not gamble. He preferred to play boules. On the night of August 9, 1976, he was watching the games in the Place Arson until 11:00 P.M., when he strolled back to his bar.

In his fifties, he had wavy black hair and suntanned good looks. He wore a white cotton shirt, navy trousers and white moccasins, and he drove a Mercedes 350. He had a criminal record, but he had kept out of trouble for many years: the police were not sure whether he had gone straight or merely got smart.

He entered the bar, greeted a few customers, and walked across to the door at the back with "Private" lettered on it in red.

Bournat was waiting in the office.

The appointment had been fixed through a boules-playing friend of Tschoa's, but the bar owner was still suspicious. He sat down and put a Dunhill cigarette into his gold cigarette holder. "What can I do for you?"

"I want to sell some gold."

"Coins or jewelry?"

"Neither,' Bournat said. "Take a look at this." He produced a gold ingot and proferred it.

Tschoa did not touch it. "How many?" he asked.

"Maybe a lot."

"What price are you asking?"

"Seventeen thousand francs per ingot."

"You bloody fool," Tschoa said contemptuously. "The market price is only a little over eighteen thousand. What do you take me for?"

"Don't get upset—I'm only a middleman—I'll inform the other party of your reaction.—"

"Tell your boss to shove it," Tschoa said angrily. He stood up and pushed back his chair. "I know perfectly well where that came from, and so does everyone in Nice. I won't touch it at any price. You're so loose-mouthed, you should put an ad in *Nice-Matin.* Now shove off, and don't come back."

BOURNAT HAD an old friend called Alfred Aimar, better known as Fred the Jeweler. In his early sixties, Fred had gone straight some fifteen years before, but he still had a few old connections. He introduced Bournat to a man who needed some fast cash.

Adrien Zeppi was not a villain. He had a small leather goods shop, but times were hard. He had remarried, to a younger woman, and they had a baby. Zeppi, aged fifty-four, was a well-respected citizen in the Plateau Flori area, but he seemed to have no objection to consorting with the likes of Fred the Jeweler. Fred marked him down as small-time.

Fred and Bournat met him in a bar in Mougins and put the proposition to him.

"We've got some gold—our life savings—and we want to cash it. But we don't have bank accounts, and anyway if we're seen selling gold, with our records there'll be all sorts of hassle . . . you know how it is. So you could do us a big favor by selling it for us. You're a respectable man, they won't question you. And we'll pay you one thousand francs per bar."

Zeppi did not hesitate. The money would be a godsend. The next day he went into his own bank, the Crédit Agricol on the N85 road between Nice and Grasse. He deposited a few checks, then casually asked the counter clerk: "I want to sell a little gold—I think I can invest in something better. Can you handle it?"

"Of course, Monsieur Zeppi. Should we deposit the money in your account?"

Zeppi hesitated. "Well, actually I would prefer to have the cash . . . you understand."

"Of course, sir. How many ingots do you want to sell?"

"Nine."

"No problem. Bring them in anytime."

Two days later Zeppi walked in with nine gold ingots—and walked out with more than thirty-two thousand dollars cash.

He met Bournat and Fred, gave them the money, and collected his seventeen-hundred-dollar commission.

Bournat was delighted. He had got the full market price for his gold, and all the others had sold it at thirty percent discount. And he had made Adrien Zeppi take the risk for him. He thought he was pretty smart.

However, gold bars are numbered, and every transaction in them is registered. Since the heist every bank in France had had a list of the numbers of the ingots stolen from the Société Générale. The teller at the Crédit Agricol checked the numbers against his list and phoned the Nice police immediately. Zeppi was tailed, and he led the detectives to Fred the Jeweler and to Alain Bournat.

MARIE FRANÇOISE Astolfi was a good deal more respectable than most of the women in this story; but she was no more discreet than Lea or Odile.

Marie was an inspector with the school meals service in Marseilles. On Saturday, October 9, 1976 she was in her apartment at Rue Charasse packing a weekend suitcase: pajamas, a toothbrush, a pants suit. Twenty-six years old, she was a well-brought-up woman who had been to boarding school. Her first job had been as a teacher. More recently other bells had been ringing for her, but good habits die hard.

Since the summer she had been in love with a tall blond man called Henri Michelucci. Two days ago he had asked her to do a favor for his brother Daniel. Daniel wanted to make a fast trip to Brussels by car, and he needed a co-driver. The round trip was more than a thousand miles, but he wanted to do it in a weekend.

Marie knew that Henri and his brother were not the most scrupulously law-abiding of men. She asked: "This trip of Daniel's—is it . . . heavy?"

"Yes, it's heavy," Henri told her.

But she liked Daniel, who was almost as good-looking as his brother; and she loved fast cars. She agreed to go.

She met Daniel in the Prado area at 1:00 P.M. on that Saturday. Following instructions, she had rented a Renault 20 from Eurocar. Daniel read *Le Soir* while she drove out of the city. After a while he told her to stop, and he disconnected the odometer to save money—the car was rented on a per-mile basis. When they drove on, he said: "Watch your speed. I don't want to be stopped by the police."

Shortly before 5:00 P.M. they stopped for a break near Villefranche sur Saône. Daniel said: "I have some people to see at Valenciennes. It might be better if you drop me there tomorrow and go on to Brussels on your own. The rooms are reserved at the President. I could join you there later in the day."

"It's your trip," she shrugged.

They spent the night in a hotel in Paris—sleeping in separate rooms. The next day they headed for the border. Marie asked: "Do you still want me to drop you at Valenciennes?"

Daniel made up his mind a few miles farther on. "No," he said. "I'll do it on the way back." Then he asked her to stop the car while he got a road map out from his suitcase.

He directed her off the main highway and on to

country roads. They got lost twice. Eventually they crossed the border at a small station in Ermitage, and reached Brussels forty-five minutes later.

Marie did not ask why Daniel was afraid to use a main border checkpoint.

First thing next morning she drove him to the Banque Lambert close to the central railway station. He went in, carrying his case. When he came out a few minutes later, he still had the case, but it was obviously a good deal lighter.

He was very cheerful over lunch. They had champagne with their dessert. Daniel leaned across the table and said in a low voice: "You know what was in my case? Gold—from the Société Générale in Nice. Not all of it, of course—I couldn't have got it all into the safe-deposit box."

Marie could not sleep that night. She had not suspected the Michelucci brothers of being big-time gangsters. Alone in her hotel room, she confided her fears to her diary.

She checked out of the hotel early the next morning, leaving a note for Daniel that said simply: "*Ciao.*" She drove very fast. She stopped in Lyons for a break and then again just outside Marseilles to reconnect the odometer cable.

Eurocar was paid for one hundred seventy miles instead of more than a thousand.

And Marie Françoise Astolfi left her diary in the car.

MARIE WAS a late addition to the list of names in Albert Mouray's office. He had been ready to pounce long before October. In fact, on Friday, August 13, he had decided that the net was spread sufficiently wide, and he had set the date for the next Monday, August 16. But over that weekend something happened that made him wonder whether his investigation was on a completely wrong track.

Spaggiari and the CIA

8

"SEWER RATS" STRIKE IN PARIS
—headline in *Nice-Matin,* 18 August 1976 (freely translated)

OVER THE weekend of August 14 and 15, a branch of the Société Générale on the Ile St. Louis in Paris was robbed. The break-in was a carbon copy of the Nice robbery.

The gang had got in through the sewers. They dug a three-yard-long tunnel from the drain to the wall of the vault, then made a hole in the reinforced concrete of the wall. To keep the air in the tunnel fresh they used an extractor similar to the one used in Nice. They used a laser to open the safe-deposit boxes in the strong room. They opened one hundred and thirty of the one hundred and ninety-one boxes.

There *was* an alarm system in this vault, and it did go off. Two security guards arrived in response to the alarm. Seeing nothing amiss, they decided that the alarm had gone wrong, and did no more.

One irony of the incident was that the insurers had negotiated a new contract with Société Générale since the Nice heist—but the contract did not become effective until August 28.

Two detectives from Nice were sent to Paris to assist the metropolitan force. Paris was convinced that the same gang had done both jobs, and they insisted that Albert Mouray hold off his sweep while they investigated.

However, as the inquiry proceeded, the theory that one gang had done both jobs seemed less and less tenable.

The Paris gang had been sloppy. Several of them had been seen, and witnesses picked them out of the police file of photographs of known criminals. The Nice robbers had left behind not one shred of useful evidence, but this was not so in Paris. The tools used in Nice had been predominantly commonplace items like hammers and chisels, but a laser had been used in Paris. (At this stage the police did not know that Spaggiari had bought a laser but had been unable to use it.)

Then there was the psychology of the matter. The Nice gang had got away with a haul worth—at the lowest estimate*—$6.2 million dollars: was it likely that they would risk their necks on another job before they had had time to spend the money?

The argument went on. It could not be a copycat crime, Paris said, for it had taken place exactly four weeks after the Nice job, and that was not enough time to plan this kind of robbery. And it was too much to believe that the same brilliant idea had occurred to two completely separate criminal brains at approximately the same time.

But Albert Mounay was getting extremely nervous. Every day that passed made it more likely that one of the people he was having followed—there were now more than forty—would spot the surveillance and spread the alarm. Then the birds would fly.

At last Paris made an arrest. Raimond Brisacier, a garage owner, was caught trying to sell one of the gold ingots stolen from the Ile St. Louis bank. The Nice suspects were observed closely for a reaction. They seemed oblivious. Therefore, there were two separate gangs.

Paris gave the green light, and Mouray set a new date: October 26.

DURING THIS two-month delay, Spaggiari was traveling.

He went to Guatemala. Then he went to the USA.

*This is the bank's estimate. For reasons which are discussed later, it must be regarded as a minimum.

He was looking for a hotel or a restaurant to buy. While he was there, he contacted the CIA.

(This sounds strange to Europeans, for here one cannot simply *contact* one's national espionage organization. Few members of the public even know where the headquarters of the Deuxième Bureau or MI5 are. However, in the USA it is as easy to contact the CIA as the electric company; and if you call the Secret Service they pick up the phone and say: "Secret Service").

Spaggiari had offered to work for the CIA. "With my organization, I can pull anything," he boasted. "No matter where, no matter what. I can open any safe, get into any embassy . . ."

America's spies were a nervous bunch at the time. They had had a very bad press during the Watergate scandal. They asked Albert how they were supposed to know he wasn't some kind of nutcase, anyway.

"What if I told you I pulled the heist of the century —the robbery of the Société Générale bank at Nice? Would that be enough?"

Like spies everywhere, the CIA are none too fastidious about who they use to acquire intelligence. But they—like the Marseilles Mob, like the Commando Delta of the OAS, like Pierre Lagaillarde—mistrusted Albert Spaggiari. It was the story of his life.

However, they played the Franco-American cooperation game, and sent to Interpol a résumé of the meeting. Sometime in September, Interpol routinely passed the report to the Nice police.

Who did nothing.

And this is the second mystery surrounding the Nice police's handling of this case.

Later, a police spokesman said: "There was no proof. Anyway, at that time we were deluged with information, nearly all of it false."

This excuse is laughable. Spaggiari had served two long jail sentences, and had been suspected of involvement in several other crimes. The Nice police were presented with a *witnessed confession.* Yet they did not pick Spaggiari up; they did not question him to see whether he had an alibi; they did not put him on the list of suspects to be followed; and they did not arrest him in the October 26 sweep. Where Albert Spaggiari was concerned they seemed to be blind, deaf and dumb.

Also, during this period Spaggiari and his wife went on a trip to Japan with the mayor of Nice.

The mayor, Jacques Médecin, was also minister of tourism in Giscard d'Estaing's government. Under his auspices the towns of Nice and Cannes and the state of Monaco organized a traveling exhibition to tour Japan and promote the Côte d'Azur. They took with them art treasures from local museums: paintings by Chagall, Matisse, Lèger and Fragonard; sculptures by Giacometti; glass by Biot. They also took generous samples of local produce like Provençal wine and olive oil; plus a team of mannequins to display French *haute couture.* They chartered a Boeing 707, but it was bigger than they needed. The extra places on the trip were sold for seven thousand francs ($1,450) each—a bargain. Spaggiari bought two.

Médecin was at pains to explain, a few weeks later, that the Spaggiaris had traveled as private individuals and had no role to play in the traveling exhibition. He told the authors that he had not even seen Spaggiari on the aircraft, and the couple had not stayed in the same hotels as the official party. On this occasion Spaggiari was not acting as mayoral photographer. He added: "It is in the nature of an intelligent criminal to hide his true character behind a façade of honesty."

The plane left on October 6, and flew via Paris and Anchorage to Tokyo. The official party stayed at the Imperial Hotel, and the Spaggiaris checked into the Hilton. One of the journalists on the trip said: "They were enthusiastic tourists, and they behaved like honeymooners. Albert looked after Audi, making sure she never went anywhere alone, always giving her little presents. They seemed to be very much in love."

On October 16 they went on to Hong Kong, staying at the Mandarin. Albert bought three suits for himself and a necklace of black pearls for Audi. Three days later they went on to Bangkok, flying over the Mekong Delta en route. Spaggiari was seized by nostalgia for his days as a paratrooper in Vietnam. "The entire four years in Indochina came back to me," he told people. "There was a knot in my throat and tears in my eyes."

They sunbathed by the pool of the Siam Intercontinental Hotel, and saw hundreds of pagodas with thousands of Buddhas. They did the rounds of antique shops, jewelry stores and silk merchants.

On October 24 they returned to Nice via New Delhi, Teheran and Tel Aviv.

Did Spaggiari have an ulterior motive for taking the trip? The Japanese newspaper *Mainichi* suggested that he had sold gold and jewelry in Tokyo and bought works of art with the cash. Certainly, if he wanted to take stolen jewelry out of France, perhaps his best chance of avoiding a customs search was to travel with the mayor of Nice.

TWO DAYS after the Spaggiaris' return to Nice, Albert Mouray and his men swooped down.

Spaggiari is Arrested

9

Bert is not a man to let his feelings show in his face.

—Audi Spaggiari

CHIEF OF Police Albert Mouray was good at this sort of thing.

The swoop involved more than five hundred policemen and gendarmes in eight towns. Forty suspects were to be seized at precisely the same moment: 6:30 A.M. on Tuesday, October 26, 1976.

Clear, precise orders went out to Marseilles, Antibes, Mougins, Toulon, Nîmes, Paris and Ajaccio in Corsica, as well as Nice. The arresting officers had names, addresses and descriptions, and in most cases had been following the suspects for some time. Every arrest was covered by a warrant. It was like a space launch at Cape Kennedy, someone said.

By lunchtime all the reports were on Albert Mouray's desk, and he was wondering what he had done wrong.

For a start, five of the forty had slipped the net: they simply had not been where they were expected to be at 6:30 that morning. Included in that five was the biggest fish of all, Dominique Poggi.

Poggi was born February 16, 1926 in Corsica. For many years he was right-hand man to Barthelemy Guerini, the French Mafia boss, and during this period only had one minor conviction—for pimping in Strasbourg in 1950. When Guerini's empire collapsed Poggi moved to Antibes, and with his brother opened the Club 62. But he was still keeping bad company: in 1972 the gunman Gavin Coppolani was arrested there. Coppolani was a most undesirable character. Three years later he escaped and tried to revenge himself on the informers who had given him away: he was himself wounded in the ensuing shoot-out, and the man who wounded him was murdered in Nice in 1976 and left on the steps of his nightclub. The fleshy-faced, sharp-suited Poggi had both the contacts and the experience of organized crime to conduct an enterprise like the heist of the century. He was the favorite for the title of *Le Cerveau*—The Brain. But he was not at home when the police called.

There was worse news to come. Twenty-seven of the thirty-five who were at home had been cleared by the end of the day, and had to be released.

It was an inevitable consequence of the way the names had been collected that some of the suspects would turn out to be innocent people who had done no more than meet a prime suspect on several occasions during the surveillance. But twenty-seven out of the thirty-five was a very disappointing failure rate.

Typical was the case of the musical instrument salesman from Béziers. The first time the gendarmes of the Plan du Var brigade went to the villa in Castagniers, they had noted the number of a metallic-gray Peugeot 504 parked in the garage. It was gone by evening, when they called a second time and found four men waiting on the steps. The gendarmes checked the registration number of the car, and traced it to the musical instrument salesman. The man was arrested at 6:30 A.M. on October 26 in Capestang, Hérault. He did indeed have a Peugeot 504, but it was white, not gray, and he was able to prove that on July 9 he had been many miles away from Castagniers. The Peugeot at the villa had had false plates, and the terrified musical instrument salesman was the innocent but unlucky victim of coincidence.

Finally, the eight people detained were no great catch.

Emile Buisson had an alibi for the weekend of the heist, but in the excitement he confessed to embezzling ten thousand francs ($2,100) from his boss.

Homer Filippi was the son of Philippe Filippi, boxing promoter and manager of world champion Marcel Cerdan. Homer was a small-time dope dealer who had contacts with the four men at the villa in Castagniers, but he could not be positively connected with the heist, and he was charged merely with possessing a firearm without a license.

Huguette Cruchendeau was a Marseilles prostitute who had done no more than associate with the associates of the Castagniers four; but the association was close enough for her to be held.

Henri Michelucci had borrowed the Renault 17 seen at the villa in Castagniers; but he claimed his brother Daniel had been driving it at the time, and Daniel was among the five who slipped the net.

Alfred "Fred the Jeweler" Aimar and Adrien Zeppi, the crook who sold stolen gold at his own bank, could be positively nailed, but only for dishonest handling.

That accounted for six of the eight detainees.

Mouray ended up with only two who were definitely Sewer Rats: Francis Pellegrin and Alain Bournat.

All things considered, it was a pretty bad day.

THE POLICE interrogation that night concentrated on Pellegrin and Bournat. Both men were fools, as has already been mentioned; and this was fortunate for the police. The shirt-sleeved detectives in the Avenue Foch went into an old and familiar routine: "We already know everything, so why don't you make it easier for yourself and confess?" Then they added:

"All your friends have made full statements, implicating you—what's the point of holding out?"

Incredibly, they fell for it.

We said earlier that the petty crooks Spaggiari recruited to help him execute his plan would be his downfall; and this is what happened.

Both Pellegrin and Bournat made complete confessions and named, as the brain who had organized the heist, Albert Spaggiari.

THE NAME was familiar to Commissaire Principal Claude Besson, Mouray's deputy. On July 31, 1974 at 10:50 A.M. a well-dressed man had entered the Banque de Paris et des Pays Bas in Nice and asked to open his safe-deposit box. A clerk accompanied him to the vault, where another customer was waiting with a gun. They tied up the clerk, who was the only employee in the bank at that time, and broke into one of the safes. They knew exactly which one they wanted: it was numbered 199, and it contained the bank's entire reserves of gold ingots. The two men put the gold—weighing one hundred and sixty-five pounds and worth more than three hundred fifty thousand dollars—into a case and disappeared. During the ensuing investigation Claude Besson's prime suspect had been Albert Spaggiari, but nothing had been proved. However, as a candidate for the title of The Brain he was quite plausible. Besson picked up the phone.

Spaggiari is Arrested

AT 11:00 P.M. on Wednesday October 27, 1976 a blond woman of about forty entered the La Vallière photography shop at 56 Route de Marseilles in Nice and asked for Monsieur Spaggiari.

André Devésa, the manager, said: "He's not here. Can I help you?"

"This is his shop, isn't it?"

"He owns it, but I've been renting it from him for six months."

"He still lives in the flat over the shop, surely?"

"No, he moved out."

"Do you know where I can get hold of him?"

"Right now? No. But he comes here regularly. I'm expecting him later today. Can I give him a message?"

"No, I want to see him personally. Is his wife still a nurse?"

"Yes. She's not here either. She's standing in for a friend."

"All right. Thank you."

"No trouble."

Devésa thought nothing of the incident. He did not see the woman get into a blue Renault with three policemen outside the shop.

Albert and Audi came into the shop later in the morning. Devésa told them of the visitor, and Albert said: "I really have no idea who that could have been."

He used the phone in the shop to order some chicken feed for his farm, then took his wife across the road for lunch in the Roi du Yan spaghetti house.

They were joined for coffee by Jean Yves Goutron, an old comrade who had been a paratrooper in Vietnam with Albert, and who retained a slight limp as a souvenir of these days. The Spaggiaris began telling him about their trip to the Far East.

Spaggiari was talking about the market in Hong Kong when a waiter interrupted him. "Monsieur Spaggiari, there is a lady outside asking for you."

Albert frowned, shrugged, and laid his cigar in the ashtray. "Perhaps it's the mystery woman from this morning," he said. "Excuse me."

He went outside and approached the woman. He was immediately surrounded by detectives and bundled into a car. It happened very fast.

A friend saw the incident and shouted: "Audi, someone's kidnapped Bert!"

A terrified Audi phoned the police to report the kidnapping. She was told that her husband had been arrested, not kidnapped; and incidentally, the police would be grateful if she could drop by to answer some questions herself.

The interrogation of Albert Spaggiari began at 2:30 P.M. on October 27.

THIS IS the most astonishing part of the story of the heist of the century, and it forms the third and most baffling of the mysteries surrounding the case.

A police sweep involving five hundred officers and

thirty-five arrests in eight towns cannot be kept secret for long. On Tuesday night it was the main topic of conversation in the bars and restaurants of the Old Town of Nice. On Wednesday morning *Nice-Matin* carried the story.

The public was not to know that the operation had very limited success. As far as Nice was concerned, the police had caught the Sewer Rats.

Spaggiari must have known about the sweep. Friends, wives and girlfriends of those arrested would have spread the word, even if the press had not. It is likely that he knew by seven A.M. on Tuesday.

Yet he did nothing.

He might have tried to leave the country—he would have got away. If that were too drastic, he might have moved into a hotel or a friend's house to lie low for a while.

But he drove into Nice, went to his shop, then took his wife to a restaurant where he was known to be a regular. He could not have made it easier for the police to pick him up, short of walking into 1 Avenue Foch in person.

It is possible that he did not know exactly who had been arrested; in which case he clearly needed to take precautions against a betrayal. Alternatively, he may have known that the wooden-headed *demi sels* Pellegrin and Bournat had been picked up; in which case he had even more reason to worry. But he did not even prepare an alibi.

Maybe he wanted to be arrested.

Or perhaps he thought for some reason that he was invulnerable?

He was interrogated non-stop for thirty-seven hours.

And all he said was: 'No.'

His inquisitors took turns to break off for rest, coffee and sleep, but Albert had none of these. Patiently, phlegmatically, he answered their questions, ignored their promises of a light sentence in exchange for co-operation, smiled at their threats.

"He is as cold as ice," remarked Claude Besson, the unimpressionable man who continued to be impressed with Spaggiari.

They showed him the CIA dossier with his confession.

"I lied," he said calmly.

Twenty policemen accompanied by Audi searched the farmhouse in Bézaudun. The house was clean except for a box of Don Miguel cigars and a case of Margnat Village wine. Outside, hidden beneath a hen coop, they found a small cache of arms: guns, thousands of rounds of ammunition, and a quantity of dynamite. They covered every square foot of the grounds with a metal detector, and turned up only old tools, rusty iron bars and tin cans. No gold.

It was not what they wanted, but it was enough to charge Albert with illegal possession of firearms. Then, at 4:00 A.M. on Friday morning, someone had the bright idea of charging Audi as an accessory, and Albert cracked. Faced with the prospect that his darling Audi would be clapped in jail on his account, he made a deal with the police: leave her alone and I'll confess.

The deal did not include naming his accomplices or returning the loot. Nevertheless, Albert Mouray and Claude Besson were pleased. The catastrophe of Tuesday turned into a victory on Friday. They had captured The Brain.

SPAGGIARI WAS brought before the examining magistrate, Judge Richard Bouazis, on Saturday October 30. A large crowd gathered outside the Palais de Justice in Nice: reporters, photographers, film crews, television cameramen and curious members of the public.

Spaggiari loved it. He revelled in the publicity. Smartly dressed, looking confident and unrepentant, he smiled, waved and gave quotes to reporters. "No, no regrets," he said into a microphone.

A friend grabbed his sleeve and whispered a hurried message: "Don't worry about Audi—we'll take care of her."

Inside the courthouse, Spaggiari talked nonstop. He bragged about his brilliance, he told of the hardships of working in the sewers, he exaggerated the value of the haul. But he said nothing of any use to the police.

"I did not act for personal gain," he said. "I carried out a military operation. I am proud to be a member of the Catena." Catena was a branch of the OAS that specialized in helping fugitives escape from the police, but it was generally believed to have disbanded after the 1958–60 period. "I did not keep one penny of my share of the loot. The money went to help the oppressed people of Yugoslavia, Portugal and Italy.

"You can't begin to imagine what we found in the vault. The value of the jewels by far surpassed the gold and the cash.

"We were constantly in touch with the outside world. We had two sets of lookouts: one to watch for the police—we knew exactly when the security patrols were passing—and one to keep an eye on the water level in the drains."

The police had wondered why the gang opened so few safe-deposit boxes, and guessed that the storm on the afternoon of Sunday July 18 may have increased the water level in the drains to the point at which the gang felt in danger of being flooded out, causing them to leave early. Not so, said Spaggiari. "We knew exactly how high the water was and we knew we were in no danger. The reason we did not open more boxes was that it took longer than I anticipated to get through the vault wall."

When he parted from the team after the heist, they all had said: "Thank you, *monsieur le directeur.*"

"The tunnel seemed to take forever to dig. We

worked at it every night until the street cleaners came."

IT RAPIDLY became clear that Spaggiari could keep this sort of thing up indefinitely. And he did. All through the winter of 1976–77 he went before Judge Bouazis once a week, on Thursday afternoons, for questioning. The judge would remind him, every so often, that the object of the exercise was to produce information of use to the police. He would tell Spaggiari he did not believe this story about the money having been given away. He would warn that Spaggiari's refusal to name names inevitably meant a longer jail sentence. Spaggiari responded with a varying mixture of boasting, vagueness, evasions and lies.

The court ran out of money. (The way in which the French judicial system is financed is, to say the least, unusual.) A loan of twenty-five hundred dollars was arranged—appropriately, with the Société Générale.

There were a few more arrests. Marie Françoise Astolfi was picked up on the strength of what she had written in her diary. Daniel Michelucci and Michele Seaglio were also held. They claimed to have been at the casino at Aix-en-Provence over the weekend of the heist, and Daniel said he had bought the gold ingots from a stranger in Italy. A few more ingots were found, along with a coin press, in a police raid on a house in Marseilles.

Dominique Poggi, who was being sought by the entire French police force, gave himself up in Athens on November 1, having audaciously made an appointment by telephone two days earlier. A blond woman in a leopard-skin coat drove him to the police station on the Boulevard Albert I in a white Simca Matra. A dark, wavy-haired man in his fifties, he was dressed for the occasion in a beige velvet suit. The girl, a well-bred Swiss socialite, drove back to their apartment in Juan les Pins alone.

Poggi denied everything.

"On the weekend of the heist I was at home in Farinole, Corsica. A whole bunch of witnesses can testify to that. I went to the villa in Castagniers for a party. If the house was headquarters for the Sewer Rats, this is the first I've heard of it. Spaggiari? Never heard of him."

But Francis Pellegrin had said he had introduced Poggi to Spaggiari, and Poggi was charged with robbery and sent to the prison in Nice where the gang was being held. However, Pellegrin later changed his testimony. "The police kept on at me. Poggi, Poggi, always Poggi. Admit it, they said: admit that Poggi is the one. Finally I told them what they wanted to hear, just to get them off my back. But in fact it was someone else I introduced to Spaggiari—a guy I met in a bar." He would not name the man he met in the bar.

The case dragged on. Spaggiari agreed to write his memoirs for the publisher of *Papillon.* His friends told interviewers that he was incapable of stealing for personal gain. "He is not interested in money. He has intelligence, guts and nerves of steel; but he always has to be in charge—has to be the one who gives the orders." His mother said she couldn't believe it, little Bert had always been such a good boy. Audi said she had not even guessed what was going on; but then, she added, Albert would never have compromised her by telling her.

The head of the Nice sewers department, Monsieur Testan, gave evidence. He had once dug a tunnel just like Spaggiari's, he said: it was the toughest job he had ever done. "There were five of us and we only managed a yard a day. One could only dig for ten minutes at a time: in such a small space you can hardly use your forearms, and you have to make do with small tools. It is extremely difficult." There was no mistaking the note of admiration in his voice.

The tourists who had accompanied Albert and Audi to Japan were flabbergasted. "Who would have thought that such a nice, polite, helpful, well-educated man could be the brain behind the bank robbery?"

In his cell, Spaggiari exercised twice a day to keep fit. His attorney, Maître Jacques Peyrat, said: "He is missing his wiffe, but his spirit is not broken. He longs for freedom, and thinks about it all the time. Sometimes he is like a child."

Security grew slack at those Thursday afternoon sessions. Spaggiari was guarded by just two officers. He regularly spent five minutes talking to Audi in the corridor outside the courtroom. The authors spoke to him there: he told us he had begun to write his memoirs.

The police were sure Spaggiari would crack eventually. He was only prolonging his own agony. In the end he would tell everything, then they would round up the rest of his accomplices and close the case. They were in no hurry. Albert Mouray was a patient man.

On Thursday March 10, 1977 the bottom dropped out of his world.

Spaggiari "Knowingly Destroys a Vehicle"

10

QUE CACHE L'ÉTERNEL
SOURIRE D'ALBERT
SPAGGIARI?
(What Is Hidden Behind Albert Spaggiari's
Eternal Smile?)
—headline in *Nice-Martin,* 3 November 1976

THE PRISONER looked pale, and he had not touched his lunch. He had had little appetite for several days now. "I don't feel too good," he told the warder. "I've been smoking too much."

The warder, whose name was Verrauld, treated Spaggiari with great respect. "Can I get you anything else, monsieur?" he asked charitably.

"No, nothing, thank you."

Verrauld left and Spaggiari got up to look at himself in the mirror. Today of all days he had to act normal: smile, joke, appear confident and carefree. It was just another Thursday afternoon, and his twentieth session in front of the examining magistrate would be just like the other nineteen—up to a point.

He dressed in his favorite black suit and white silk shirt, and stuck the usual Don Miguel cigar in the corner of his mouth. When they came for him at precisely 2:30 P.M. he smiled, greeted the policemen and held out his hands for the cuffs.

He was driven in a gray-green prison van from the jail to the Palais de Justice. The usual two police motorcycles followed the van, plus—unknown to Spaggiari—an extra escort of four detectives in an unmarked car. Judge Richard Bouazis had ordered additional security only two weeks previously.

Spaggiari walked from the van up the marble steps of the courthouse, handcuffed to one policeman, held gently but firmly by the arm by a second. Both guards were armed. He took the steps two at a time, making his guards keep up with him, showing off his fitness. He spoke familiarly to them.

The courtroom was very small, with a worn linoleum floor and faded yellow-gray paint. There were no curtains at the window. The place was overdue for redecoration, and bars would be put in the windows at the same time; but the job had been postponed due to lack of funds.

On the right of the door was a medium-sized desk for the magistrate. Next to it was the clerk of the court's table, piled high with documents. There were four chairs and an ashtray.

Spaggiari walked in and shook hands with his attorney, Maître Jacques Peyrat, a broad-shouldered former Foreign Legionnaire who was standing for election to the town council. Peyrat was a friend of Mayor Jacques Médecin. It was Peyrat who negotiated the publishing deal for Spaggiari's memoirs.

Judge Bouazis came in. The two police guards removed Spaggiari's handcuffs and went out, locking the courtroom door from the outside.

Just four people were left inside: Spaggiari, Peyrat, Bouazis, and Mademoiselle Hoarau, a lady of around forty with a severe hairstyle, who had already typed hundreds of pages of transcript from the hearings.

The questions began. Spaggiari smoked continuously and was as evasive as ever. At 4:50 P.M. Bouazis reminded him that the previous week he had promised a detailed plan of the heist.

Slowly, Spaggiari reached inside his black velvet jacket and took out a piece of paper. He handed it to the magistrate. "*Voilà.* Here is everything you wanted to know."

Bouazis unfolded the paper. It was covered with lines, marks and inscriptions. He studied it with increasing mystification. Suddenly he looked up. "I can't make head nor tail of this. Where is the exhibition hall?"

Peyrat looked at his client at that moment, and was shocked at Spaggiari's appearance. The attorney said later: "He was absolutely white—I have never seen him so tense. He looked like a corpse. Suddenly I was very afraid for him."

Spaggiari stood up. "Don't worry," he said to the magistrate. Slowly, he walked across the tiny room, past Mademoiselle Hoarau's table and around Judge Bouazis's desk. He leaned over the magistrate's shoulder, pointed at something on the plan, and said: "Look—"

Then he leaped to the window, flung it open and jumped out.

Maître Peyrat screamed: "No, don't do it, don't do it!" ("I thought he was trying to commit suicide," he explained later.)

The magistrate and the attorney sprang from their seats and rushed to the window.

Below this particular window—which is on the second floor—there is a ledge a couple of feet wide which overhangs the high door of a side entrance to the courthouse. This entrance is called the *service étrangers,* and foreigners line up outside it every day to apply for visa extensions and conduct other business concerned with passports and residence permits. Spaggiari jumped onto this ledge.

From there he jumped onto the roof of a parked Renault 6, denting the roof.

He rolled off the roof and landed on his feet in the street.

Beside the Renault was a metallic-green Kawasaki 900 motorcycle, its engine revving. The stocky rider wore a helmet with a tinted visor. Spaggiari jumped onto the pillion.

From the window, Richard Bouazis yelled: *"Arrêtez-le! Arrêtez-le!"* (Stop him!)

Spaggiari called: *"Au revoir,"* and gave a V-sign.

Passersby heard his laughter as the motorcycle disappeared into the Boulevard Jean Jaurès.

The fugitives suffered a bad moment in the Boulevard Jean Jaurès when a car backed out of a parking lot into their path. But the motorcyclist was skilled, and he managed to swing the speeding machine around the reversing car, just touching it.

Outside the courthouse a policeman jumped onto his motorcycle and began to follow; but Spaggiari had too long a start, and the policeman lost sight of him almost immediately.

The police force reacted very quickly. Within ten minutes roadblocks were being set up all around Nice, the French border was closed, and all trains and planes out of the city were canceled. A private jet that had just taken off was ordered to land again. A massive manhunt began.

It was all to no avail.

Spaggiari had vanished.

He has not been seen since.

HE HAS, however, been heard from.

The beige Renault 6 on whose roof he landed was quite badly damaged, and had to be replaced. The owner, a Monsieur Gonzales, was heartbroken. The car was almost new. Monsieur Gonzales lived in the Rue de Pontin, near the courthouse. His brand-new car had already been damaged once, and he had parked it next to the courthouse because he thought it would be safest there.

The repair cost over six hundred dollars and Monsieur Gonzales's insurance company refused to pay out on such a bizarre accident claim. All he could do was file a complaint with the police of knowingly destroying a vehicle against one Albert Spaggiari, address unknown.

It was a funny story, and *Nice-Matin* ran it.

A few days later Gonzales received through the mail $625 in cash and a note of apology from Spaggiari.

SEVEN BOTTLES of champagne were drunk in the Roi du Yan—Spaggiari's favorite restaurant—on the night of March 10. The old comrades were celebrating.

Maître Jacques Peyrat was considerably embarrassed. "He must have planned the whole thing in advance," he said. "He led me and the examining magistrate right up the garden path."

The court officials were also embarrassed. A year earlier another prisoner had escaped through the very same window. (He had, however, been caught soon afterward in the Old Town.)

The police were embarrassed, and the government was none too pleased. Minister of the Interior Michael Poniatowski was on the phone from Paris. One thousand police officers conducted a house-to-house search in the Old Town. They also raided the farmhouse at Bézaudun—and found that Audi, too, had disappeared.

The doors were unlocked and the shutters were open, but there was nobody at home. The police interviewed neighbor Ange Goujon. "I've been feeding the dogs, Packa and Vesta, and the chickens," he said. "But I expected Madame Spaggiari to return at any moment."

Audi's nursing colleague, Mademoiselle Fabienne Nehr, said Audi had left on March 3. "She had a bad day, and I suggested she take a drive into the mountains. That was the last I saw of her."

On that day Audi had gone to the photographic shop in the Route de Marseilles carrying a small suitcase. André Devésa, who by this time had bought the shop, said: "She told us she was going away until March 25. She seemed very tired."

Spaggiari's attorney, Maître Jacques Peyrat, had also known that Audi was going away. "She was totally exhausted after all the trouble. She did not want to be bothered anymore, and she wanted to get out of Nice. Also, there had been anonymous threats against her.

She left for an unknown destination, and said she would be away for a few weeks."

Audi was, of course, the only person—other than Peyrat—who had been able to talk to Spaggiari during his internment: remember those unofficial five-minute sessions in the courthouse corridor? She must have arranged the details of the escape. Now she had vanished as completely as her husband.

The police began interviewing the witnesses to the escape. The motorcycle driver had been waiting in the Rue de la Préfecture since 1:00 P.M. He had been cleaning the spokes of his wheels. Most of the time he had been wearing the helmet with the tinted visor; but at one point he took it off, and several people got a good look at his face.

Commissaire Jacques "Colombo" Tholance gave three small cheers and dug out the file of photographs of Spaggiari's associates.

Several witnesses picked out the motorcyclist from the file.

He was Gérard Rang, twenty-eight, owner of the notorious Chi-Chi nightclub in Haut de Cagnes. He had straight blond hair and a stocky build. He was a right-wing extremist, but Tholance had a file on him as thick as the Manhattan phone book. He and Spaggiari had been jointly suspected of two crimes: a large-scale checkbook fraud that had flooded Nice with dud checks in the summer of 1974; and the slick two-man holdup of the Banque de Paris et des Pays Bas at Nice in the same year. Rang alone had been accused of running a fraudulent betting syndicate that "invested" subscribers' money in bets on sure things but never paid out.

Rang was also a client of Maître Jacques Peyrat.

And Jacques Tholance remembered that during the heist of the century a motorcyclist had been lookout at the riverbed entrance to the underground road.

On Sunday, March 13, at 10:00 A.M., Commissaire Tholance and twenty-four officers surrounded a luxury block of apartments called l'Arkadia at Mont Fabron, a hill overlooking Nice. Tholance went up to apartment 2F, overlooking the pool, and rang the bell.

He was ringing for some time before he heard a noise inside. "Open up, Rang," he shouted. "Come on out. You can't get away."

Eventually there was a reply. "Okay, I'll be down in five minutes."

Tholance recognized Rang's voice. He waited. Five minutes later Rang opened the door. He was wearing a black Yves St. Laurent blazer, gray flannel trousers and black high-heeled boots. He put on his sunglasses and came out.

He seemed very sure of himself. "Whatever you're arresting me for, you're making a mistake," he said.

Tholance made no reply. There was plenty of time for all that.

Rang's defense of himself was surprisingly weak.

First he said that he drove a 525 cc bike, and could not handle a Kawasaki 900. Nobody was impressed with this lie.

Then he produced an alibi. "I was playing tennis at the time—in the club next to l'Arkadia."

"With whom?"

"On my own."

"How does one play tennis alone?"

"Up against a wall."

Evidence was produced. One of Peyrat's colleagues arrived with four girls from l'Arkadia who testified they had seen Rang playing tennis up against a wall.

(The colleague was Martine Wolf, who was [a] Peyrat's second at the Spaggiari hearings; [b] Rang's girlfriend; and [c] the tenant of a flat at 5 Rue de la Préfecture, opposite the window from which Spaggiari had jumped.)

Rang was indeed a paid-up member of the tennis club, but nobody there could remember him using its facilities during the past twelve months. Commissaire Tholance ordered a lineup. The four girls failed to pick Rang out of the lineup. They had indeed seen someone playing solo tennis, but their window was too far from the court for them to swear that the player had been Rang.

Tholance then organized another lineup, this time for two people who had witnessed the escape. Rang was lined up with four stocky, blond policemen. Both witnesses unhesitatingly picked Rang out of the line.

Rang was charged with aiding and abetting Spaggiari's escape.

ON MARCH 19, OAS comrades of Spaggiari told the authors: "We've done it. He's out of the country."

ON MARCH 20 Jacques Peyrat was elected town councilor.

Epilogue

Bien le bonjour d'Albert!

—postcard from Spaggiari to the authors, April 1977

LESS THAN one million francs (about $214,000) of the loot was recovered: the gold Bournat tried to sell, the gold found in Daniel Michelucci's safe-deposit box in Brussels, and the gold found in the house at Marseilles.

The Société Générale claimed thirty million francs from their insurers, Lloyds. However, that may simply be the maximum they were insured for. Jacques Guenet, the manager, denies this; but no banker in his right mind would admit it even if it were true.

Secondly, the losers may not have claimed everything. One reason people rent safe-deposit boxes is to conceal their wealth from the tax man or the police. Seven people refused to deposit an inventory of the contents of their boxes, so their losses are excluded from the thirty million francs. Others may have claimed for only part of what they lost, being afraid to admit to possession of valuables that may have been stolen or cash that had not been declared to the tax authorities.

(There was one man in Nice who told anyone who would listen that the heist of the century had cost him half a million francs for just that reason. His name was Gérard Rang.)

Spaggiari himself claimed the heist netted one hundred million francs, but he exaggerated everything.

We may safely conclude that the haul was between thirty million and one hundred million; probably nearer to thirty million. Even at thirty million francs (about $6.2 million) it is the biggest bank raid of all time.

NO SATISFACTORY answers have yet emerged to the three mysteries:

Why did the Nice police not know in advance of the heist?

Why did they take no action when the CIA told them of Spaggiari's confession?

And why did Spaggiari not go into hiding after the October 26 arrests?

On its own, the third question might be answered by

saying that Spaggiari was a megalomaniac, and like most megalomaniacs he thought he led a charmed life, protected by the gods.

The trouble with that is that he *did* lead a charmed life, as the other two questions indicate. One must inevitably speculate that perhaps he *was* protected. But by whom? And why did his protectors eventually desert him, only to rescue him again?

At this point politics enters the discussion. Nice is a conservative place, with a right-wing town council. All the *dramatis personae* in this story are rightists of one kind or another, from the mayor to Gérard Rang. The people form fascinating circles: the mayor knew Spaggiari, who was an associate of Rang, whose girlfriend was Martine Wolf, who was colleague of Jacques Peyrat, who was a close friend of the mayor. (Mayor Jacques Médecin's connections with Spaggiari, tenuous and trivial though they may be, would have caused the resignation of many politicians; but the Médecins are the most powerful family in Nice, providing most of the town's mayors—Avenue Jean Médecin is named after one—and Jacques's position is too strong to be jeopardized by a whiff of scandal.) But it is the OAS that rears its ugly head most frequently in this story. Spaggiari was a member; so were some of the Sewer Rats. Spaggiari always claimed he had given his slice of the cake to the OAS. And the OAS claimed the credit for getting him out of France after the escape. Is it possible that OAS sympathizers in high places protected him from police inquiries? We can do no more than ask the question.

If he was protected, there remains the puzzle of why he permitted himself to be arrested and then escaped.

All his life Spaggiari had big ideas, but nobody would ever give him the chance to put them into practice. Now, it is possible that in the end he made his own chance, and proved that he was capable. All the evidence points that way, and that is the way we have told the story. But there is another possibility, and that is that Spaggiari was merely the lieutenant for some other, unknown criminal brain, either a master villian or a political fanatic. Allowing himself to be arrested might have been Spaggiari's way of protecting the *real* brain behind the heist. If this was so it certainly worked, for the Nice police are no longer looking for a mystery man behind the heist—they are looking for the fugitive Spaggiari.

This hypothesis, if correct, would explain one other puzzle: the carbon-copy heist at the Ile St. Louis in Paris. Discussing that, we noted that (a) it was unlikely that the same gang would take the risk of a second job before they had chance to spend the $6.2 million they netted from the Nice bank; and (b) it was equally unlikely that two completely separate gangs should at the same moment in time hit on such a similar method of robbing a bank vault. However, it is quite possible that one top criminal organizer thought of the idea and put it into practice with two separate gangs in two far-apart cities at around the same time.

Let us follow this hypothesis to its logical conclusion, remembering that all the time we are moving further from the mere facts and into the realms of sheer speculation. The real brain planned the heist, used Spaggiari as his arms and legs, and arranged high-placed protection. Then, in order to deflect attention from himself and provide the anxious public and the inquisitive police with a plausible scapegoat, he let Spaggiari be arrested. But he could not be certain that Spaggiari would hold out against interrogation forever, so he organized the rescue. What more can he now do to protect himself?

Well, he could kill Spaggiari.

IN THE autumn of 1977 a rumor circulated in Nice that Spaggiari had, indeed, been murdered. However, up to that point there was considerable evidence that he was alive and well.

He sent the authors a postcard: a picture of himself, wearing a heavy coat and a beret (perhaps to conceal an appearance-altering new hairstyle). The message on the back was: "Bien le bonjour d'Albert!" An expert calligrapher compared the message with handwriting known to be Spaggiari's and declared them identical.

He also sent to *Nice-Matin* a letter alleging that Gérard Rang had not been the motorcyclist who helped him escape.

The card, the letter, and the cash sent to the owner of the damaged Renault 6 were all posted in Nice, which probably means nothing at all.

The old comrades in the Roi du Yan spaghetti house say they know where he is. "We were able to get him out of the country with the help of our Italian friends. But he will not stay there." He and Audi are moving around, they say.

To Japan, perhaps? That is where some of his wealth is stashed, according to the Japanese press; but their guess is probably no better than anyone else's.

Or there is Guatemala, which Spaggiari visited sometime between the heist and his arrest. Guatemala has no extradition treaty with France.

Guatemala, Japan, Italy, Nice . . . we are back to speculation. He could be anywhere.

But the arm of the law is extraordinarily long, as Britain's Great Train Robbers found out.

These days, if you meet Commissaire Jacques Tholance—France's "Colombo"—in one of his favorite *louche* bars in the Old Town of Nice, he will raise his bushy eyebrows and drink to Luck. "Spaggiari is laughing," he will tell you with a self-deprecating smile. "But he who laughs last, laughs longest. To Luck."